'Your contact is over there, Dr Washington.' The flight attendant pointed in the direction of a man leaning by an old open-top Army Jeep, his arms folded over his chest, his legs crossed at the ankles. The man had dark hair, dark skin, and was dressed in khaki shorts, with a hat on his head, sunglasses covering his eyes and hiking boots on his feet.

He didn't look anything like a doctor! He looked rugged and wild and unruly.

Melora swallowed over her suddenly dry throat and looked from the man back to the attendant. '*He's* my contact? Are you sure?' He most certainly didn't look anything like a doctor. 'I'm to be met by Dr...' She stopped and dug into the pocket of her linen trousers for the piece of paper she'd printed out. 'Dr...er...' She consulted the page. 'Tarvon? Daniel Tarvon?'

Melora looked at the man who looked as though he hadn't had the opportunity to shave that morning. It gave him a dangerous but exciting look, and she couldn't stop the butterflies from churning in her stomach. This was it. She was here. Her adventure was about to begin...with a real-life jungle man as her guide.

Lucy Clark is actually a husband-and-wife writing team. They enjoy taking holidays with their children, during which they discuss and develop new ideas for their books using the fantastic Australian scenery. They use their daily walks to talk over characterisation and fine details of the wonderful stories they produce, and are avid movie buffs. They live on the edge of a popular wine district in South Australia with their two children, and enjoy spending family time together at weekends.

Recent books by the same author:

THE DOCTOR AND SOCIETY'S SWEETHEART
THE DOCTOR'S DOUBLE TROUBLE
A BABY FOR THE FLYING DOCTOR

DOCTOR: DIAMOND IN THE ROUGH

BY
LUCY CLARK

First published in Great Britain 2011
by Mills & Boon,
an imprint of Harlequin (UK) Limited,
Large Print edition 2011
Eton House, 18-24 Paradise Road,
Richmond, Surrey TW9 1SR

© Anne and Peter Clark 2011

ISBN: 978 0 263 21753 7

Harlequin (UK) policy is to use papers that are
natural, renewable and recyclable products and made
from wood grown in sustainable forests. The logging
and manufacturing process conform to the legal
environmental regulations of the country of origin.

Printed and bound in Great Britain
by CPI Antony Rowe, Chippenham, Wiltshire

DOCTOR: DIAMOND IN THE ROUGH

For my wonderful mother—Glenda—
who is a constant source of support and
inspiration and who fervently hopes that one
day I'll learn the difference between 'affect'
and 'effect'. Thank you—for everything.

CHAPTER ONE

MELORA WASHINGTON slipped her sunglasses onto her face, hefted her large carry-on bag over her shoulder and gave the flight attendant a polite smile. She stood in the doorway of the small twelve-seater Cessna, looking out into the bright Tarparniian daylight.

This was it. She'd made the decision, had done the mound of paperwork required to apply, passed the interviews, completed her medical checks and had been approved to work for Pacific Medical Aid for the next two weeks.

The need to take a break from her life as a general surgeon working at a busy teaching hospital in Sydney was something she was definitely looking forward to. Coming here, to a world so different from her own, with the promise of adventure and excitement—*anything* that was new and out of the ordinary was what she was looking for.

It had been her close friend Emerson Freeman

who had been the one to suggest Tarparnii as the 'take a break from my life' destination.

'You've been through too much in the past few years, Mel,' Emmy had implored. 'Taking a break, a complete getaway from the path your life has been forced down, would definitely benefit you.'

'Tarparnii?' Melora had been stupefied at the suggestion. 'That's a jungle. I was thinking of a nice quiet resort in Far North Queensland.'

'You'd be bored within twenty-four hours,' Emmy had pointed out. 'You've been through an emotionally draining physical experience, not to mention all the drama associated with the nullification of your engagement.'

'But a jungle?' Even the word 'jungle' had made Melora wonder whether this could really be possible.

'What could be more different from your present lifestyle here in Sydney than a jungle? Trust me. You'll love it. The people are wonderful, the scenery is to die for and PMA offers you the opportunity to help out in a practical sense. Besides, it's only for two weeks.'

Emmy had made some valid points and at that point in her life, after the upheaval she'd lived through, Melora had been almost desperate to get away, to try something different, to *be* someone different from the woman who'd felt as though the walls had been closing in on her. Her world may have been blown apart, crashing down around her in an array of disappointment, disillusionment and discouragement, but that hadn't meant she had to stand for it.

'Tarparnii will help you to heal,' Emmy had said softly. 'Trust me on this.'

Melora had looked at her friend, had seen the concern in her eyes and heard it in her voice. 'You really think it's the right thing to do?'

Emmy had smiled brightly and reached for her phone. 'I do. Let's call PMA now and get this show on the road.' As Emmy had made the phone call, Melora had felt a buzz of rejuvenation flood through her.

Could she really do this? Take more leave from the hospital, take some time out of her everyday world and try another? She'd heard Emmy and her husband, Dart, talk about Tarparnii for years but never in her wildest dreams had she thought that she, herself, would go.

Then again, she'd also thought that her future had lain with Leighton, with marrying him and starting a family, and look at how badly that had

turned out. Add that to her recent surgery and multitude of tests, and she had been more than ready
for something new.

As Emmy had finished making the phone call
to arrange an appointment for Melora to go to the
PMA offices, excitement had burst forth from her
friend. 'You'll love Tarparnii, Mel, and April is a
beautiful month to go. It's always humid and sticky
and it rains almost every day but it's still stunning. Oh, and the people you'll meet. Meeree and
Jalak are like loving, caring parents to anyone who
enters their village, and then there are the doctors
and nurses who live there, like Belhara and Bel
and Tarvon.' Emmy nodded enthusiastically. 'It'll
be great. You'll love it. I promise.'

Melora blinked, bringing her thoughts back to
the present, amazed that she was finally there,
finally taking that tenuous step away from everything she'd known in order to try something so
completely different. She smiled again at the flight
attendant in eager excitement.

'Your PMA contact is over there, Dr Washington.'
The flight attendant pointed in the direction of a
man leaning by an open-top old army Jeep, his
arms folded over his chest, his legs crossed at the
ankles. The man had dark hair, dark skin and was

dressed in khaki shorts and a pale blue striped cotton shirt, which appeared to be mis-buttoned. There was a hat on his head, sunglasses covering his eyes and hiking boots on his feet.

He didn't look anything like a doctor! He looked rugged and wild and unruly.

She swallowed over her suddenly dry throat and looked from the man back to the attendant. '*He's* my contact? Are you sure?' He most certainly didn't look anything like a doctor. 'I'm to be met by Dr…' She stopped and dug into the pocket of her linen trousers for the piece of paper she'd printed out. 'Dr…er…' She consulted the page. 'Tarvon? Daniel Tarvon?'

The attendant's eyebrows hit her hairline. 'Is that his first name? I never knew. Everyone always calls him Tarvon.'

Melora pointed to the man who looked as though he hadn't had the opportunity to shave that morning. It gave him a dangerous but exciting look and she couldn't stop the butterflies from churning in her stomach. This was it. She was here. Her adventure was about to begin…with a real-life jungle man as her guide. 'And *that's* Tarvon?'

'It is indeed, Dr Washington.' The attendant appeared to be looking at Dr Daniel Tarvon as though he was the best thing since sliced bread. The woman sighed with longing, as though she wanted nothing more than to head on over to Daniel Tarvon and press her lips eagerly to his own. Melora let her gaze rest on the overall package the man made and from where she stood she had to admit that he appeared quite trim, taut and terrific. Then again, looks weren't everything, as she'd already figured out with Leighton.

The woman beside her quickly straightened, as though only just realising she'd been caught ogling the Tarparniian doctor, cleared her throat and turned back to face Melora, a polite smile pasted in place.

'On behalf of Pacific Airways, I'd like to thank you for flying with us today, Dr Washington, and hope you have an enjoyable and safe time in Tarparnii.'

Melora nodded. 'Thanks.' Feeling her excitement bubble to the surface, she dragged in a deep breath, watching Dr Tarvon as he leaned against the old green Jeep, which appeared to have known better days...*much* better days. It was as though she'd stepped out of reality and into some strange, world with lush green trees, high humidity and relaxed doctors. She was used to the crisp efficiency of a large teaching hospital, overbooked clinics and operating lists, and doctors who wore three-piece suits. Dr Tarvon appeared to be a far cry from any of that.

Hefting her bag once more, she alighted from the plane and walked across the open tarmac towards the Jeep, which was parked next to the large shed that served as the airport's terminal. Dr Tarvon didn't move, his arms still crossed, his legs still crossed, his reflective sunglasses making it impossible for her to see his eyes.

It was now that she could see more clearly the stubble indicating he probably hadn't shaved for a few days. It also appeared that he was sporting a little ponytail and that surprised her even more. As far as a contrast to Leighton, Dr Daniel Tarvon was the complete opposite. Both were good looking but there was something about the indolent man before her that seemed to radiate sensuality.

Melora breathed it in, the warm humid Tarparniian air filling her senses along with an earthy, muscular scent from the man before her. He was much taller than he'd looked from the doorway of the plane. Probably about six feet four inches. Far taller than the average Tarparniian, or, at least, so her research had led her to believe. After her initial meeting with PMA, Melora had spent quite a bit of time researching the island, its customs and its people. While she might be looking for a change, for a bit of adventure, she also liked to be prepared.

Even though she stood right in front of Dr Tarvon, he still didn't move. Arms crossed, legs crossed, reflective glasses shining her image back to her. She'd dressed with the humid climate in mind, wearing a pair of comfortable walking boots, linen trousers and a large cotton shirt, tied with a scarf at her neck. She'd read about the large sandflies and ticks and other insects Tarparnii was infamous for and was eager to avoid them wherever possible. She'd been poked and prodded enough during the past twenty months to last her a lifetime and she knew there was still more to come. The last thing she needed now was to get sick during her time there.

She continued to stand there, feeling highly self-conscious, and Dr Tarvon's silence making her rather apprehensive. Perhaps he wasn't her contact? Perhaps the flight attendant had been wrong? She looked around but there really was no one else about.

'Hello?' When he didn't immediately respond,

she began to wonder if he really was all right. She reached out a finger, edging closer, and gave him a little poke in his upper arm. 'Hello?' she said at the same time, her tone a little louder.

'Huh? What?' Dr Tarvon jolted as though she'd startled him. He sprang upright, knocking his hat from his head, his sunglasses skewing slightly. 'What? Oh. Sorry. Must have dozed off. Rough night.' His tone was deep and his words were crisp, indicating a strong British accent, which surprised her given Emmy had led her to believe he was a native Tarparniian. Dr Tarvon bent to pick up his hat and shifted his sunglasses to the top of his head before holding out his hand to her, a tired yet jovial smile on his face. 'Dr Washington?'

'Yes.' She took off her sunglasses so she could greet him properly.

'I'm Tarvon.'

'Daniel Tarvon?' Melora confirmed, slipped her hand into his, noting the way his large, warm hand seemed to envelop hers completely. He really was tall, dark and handsome and just the brief touch of her skin against his was enough to give her a tingle of awareness.

'Yes. Great to meet you.' He actually shook her hand, up and down, rather than a polite clasping squeeze as she was used to back home. 'Actually,' he continued, letting her hand go for a brief moment before clasping both of hers in his, 'we should greet like this.' He moved their hands in small circles and she experienced the traditional Tarparniian welcome that she'd read about on line.

'Yes. Of course. When in Tarparnii…' She let the sentence hang as she tried to calm the way her body seemed to have become electrified by his touch.

He chuckled as he slowly let go of her hands. 'Exactly.' Her skin had been so soft, so tender and so completely different from his own callused hands. 'OK, then.' He took his hat off and tossed it into the back seat of the old Jeep, which she now saw had several rust spots, a broken taillight, no rear-vision mirror, and the corner of the front windscreen held together with some sticking tape. 'Ready to go?' He stepped forward and took the bag from her shoulder, placing it into the Jeep with ease. 'Or do you have more luggage to come?'

As he moved towards her, she caught a glimpse of something hanging off the belt at his waist. Her eyes widened as she realised it was a sheathed hunting knife. A knife? She was about to get in a car with a man who had a knife strapped to his waist.

'Dr Washington?' he prompted, and she immediately lifted her gaze from the knife to meet his. 'Any other luggage?'

'Er…no. That's it.'

'Excellent.' He noticed her gaze drop back to the hunting knife and saw her wariness at getting into a car with him. He couldn't blame her. He was sure that in Sydney not many people walked around with hunting knives on their belts. He put his hand on the knife then looked at her. 'Out here, we use these for protection. There are a lot of predators, such as poisonous snakes, *ha'kuna*—which is like a cross between a dog and a wolf—and other nasties, roaming in the jungle.' He patted his knife. 'It is a necessity.'

Melora, somewhat appeased by his explanation, nodded. 'Fair enough.'

Daniel indicated the passenger side. 'I'd hold the door open for you if there was one but as there isn't, please have a seat.'

Melora eyed the vehicle. 'Are you sure it's going to hold together long enough to transport us to where ever it is we're going?'

He laughed, a rich, deep sound that washed over her with delight. 'I'm sure.'

She sat down and held up a piece of thick rope. 'And this is?'

'Your seat belt. Even though it doesn't look like much, it will do the job of keeping you secure as we drive along.'

'Really?' Her lips twitched in disbelief.

'Really. We'll be encountering some rather rocky terrain between here and the village.'

'OK. I'll take your word for it.' She did as he'd suggested, positive that this particular car had been used in the Second World War it was so decrepit. Dr Tarvon came around to the driver's side, touched two wires together to start the engine, and after they'd both put their sunglasses back on turned to look at her again.

'Ready?'

She grinned at him and nodded, holding on to the side of the front windscreen as the car jolted into motion, the excitement at her jungle adventure actually beginning bubbling through her.

The buildings of the small Tarparniian town that straddled the airport disappeared within the blink of an eye and before she knew it, they were driving along a dirt road, lots of lush green trees surrounding them. The scenery was beautiful and very soothing.

As they drove along, Dr Tarvon had continued to impress her further by pointing out different areas of interest and giving her details of his country.

'Have you lived here long?' she found herself asking, mildly intrigued by him. He most certainly didn't fit into the mental picture she'd drawn of the typical Tarparniian, given that he was taller, broader and had that exciting rugged edge to him.

'I was born here, although educated in England.'

Well, that explained his accent and the fact that he was a qualified medical doctor. Her friends Emmy and Dart had had nothing but praise for Daniel Tarvon but Melora was eager to make up her own mind, although he was most definitely off to a good start. If she had to work alongside this handsome colleague during her time here, that would be a hardship she'd just have to bear.

She was here for adventure. She was here for an escape from reality, an escape from her life, and while she knew nothing serious would ever happen between herself and her new colleague, or any of her colleagues for that matter, it was great just to let loose and step outside her comfort zone.

After a pause, Dr Tarvon asked, 'What's your first name, Dr Washington?'

'Oh. Sorry. You don't know? I would have presumed it was on the paperwork PMA sent.'

Daniel's smile was instantaneous and natural. 'It most probably was, Dr Washington, but unfortunately I didn't have much time to prepare for your arrival. You see, we spent most of yesterday in a clinic on the other side of the island. We only arrived back in the village two hours ago. I had just enough time to have a quick wash before driving out to the airport to meet you.'

'Oh. Do you often travel to the other side of the island?'

'Yes. Quite often. Luckily, for you, the rest of today is considered as time off so you'll have the opportunity to settle in and relax before tomorrow, when we'll take you to the waterhole, throw you in and see if you swim.'

'Swim?' Melora's eyes widened in absolute horror, her mouth went dry and nervous heat settled over her. She swallowed. 'I'm afraid I don't swim, Dr Tarvon. In fact, I didn't even pack a bathing suit.' Of course she *could* physically swim but given that she'd had major surgery, her body shape changing drastically, she didn't feel at all comfortable with the concept.

Daniel looked over at her for a moment before a wide grin split his face and he chuckled. 'I didn't mean it literally, Dr Washington. I simply meant we have a long clinic day ahead of us tomorrow. It'll be extremely hectic but I'm sure you'll do fine.'

'Oh.' Melora closed her eyes, glad she was still wearing her sunglasses so he couldn't see the embarrassment written all over her face. She took a few deep breaths, forcing herself to relax, to let go of the tension that had instantly gripped her at the thought of swimming. Although she was here for adventure, there were some things she needed to leave until later…such as after her breast reconstruction surgery.

'But it is a shame you don't swim. The waterhole is lovely this time of year, Dr Washington—and you still haven't told me your first name. We're very informal out here,' he continued. 'There's no room for Dr this or Mr that.'

'My name is Melora.'

'Melora,' he repeated, and then smiled, his straight white teeth gleaming in the midmorning sunlight. 'A very pretty name.'

'Thank you.' Although she couldn't see his eyes, she was surprised and a little touched at his words. No man had ever said that to her before. 'It was my aunt's name. She died not long after I was born.' Now, why had she just told him that?

Usually, she didn't volunteer personal information until she knew people a lot better rather than the twenty minutes she'd known Dr Tarvon. Still, there was something about him, perhaps his easy-going nature combined with his jovial humour, that made her feel more relaxed in his presence.

'I'm named after my father.'

For the first time since they'd met, Melora detected the veiled hint of censure in his words. Was it his name he didn't like or was it the mention of his father? 'The flight attendant on the plane didn't know your first name. She said she only knew you as Tarvon. Emmy and Dart always referred to you as Tarvon as well.'

He raised an interested eyebrow. 'Ah...you know Emmy and Dart. Great. They're such wonderful people and they do always call me Tarvon. Most people around here do. My mother is Tarparniian and my father was British. When I'm in England, which isn't very often, I'm known as Daniel. Here, I'm usually known as Tarvon.'

She thought on this for a moment. 'Tarvon sounds like a Tarparniian name. Am I right?'

'Correct. Tarvon is my mother's family name.' He passed on the information but could see in advance where this conversation might lead.

'Oh. So even though your father was English, is it the Tarparniian custom that any children take the mother's surname?' She hadn't read about that in her research but, then, she doubted the internet covered *everything* about this magnificent country.

Daniel clenched his jaw but kept his smile in place. 'No. My father's surname is Knightsbridge but as we never got along, when I was old enough, I legally took my Tarparniian ancestral name.'

She absorbed this information, realising it told her a lot about the relationship he'd shared...or more correctly *hadn't* shared...with his father. 'You took the trouble to change your name and yet you didn't change your first name—the name that was the same as your father's?'

'My mother was the one to name me Daniel and she is the one I kept it for.'

Melora nodded, hearing the softer tone in his voice when he spoke of his mother.

'You're close to her? Your mother?'

His natural smile returned to his face. 'I am.'

'That's nice. Do you have any siblings?'

'Yes. Two sisters. You are certainly full of questions, Melora Washington.'

'Sorry. I'm not usually this nosy about my colleagues. I simply find your country and its customs extremely interesting. I apologise if I've caused you any discomfort.'

'It's fine.' He waved her words away, his tone more calm and relaxed, as it had been when they'd first met. 'Question away. If you get too personal, I'll let you know.'

'OK. So, Dr Tarvon, tell me how long have you been working with PMA?'

'Many years—far too many to count. I am a permanent member of their Tarparniian staff. Unlike you and a lot of other doctors who volunteer to come and help here for a period of time, as I'm classified as a native Tarparniian, I don't have time restrictions placed on me.'

'I see.' There was silence for a few minutes before she asked, 'So...do I call you Daniel or Tarvon?'

Daniel slowed the vehicle and turned off the graded road into what appeared to be a very loose track. 'Take your pick. Which do you prefer?'

Melora thought for a moment, feeling quite strange at being able to choose what she would call this man who was her main contact. Choosing to call him Tarvon might help to keep things on a more medical footing. However, he'd already told her that out here they were all very informal and, therefore, it might actually be better to call him by the name his mother liked. Besides, he *looked* like a Daniel.

'I like Daniel,' she finally decided.

'You gave that a bit of thought.'

'Why wouldn't I? It was an important decision. After all, you are the PMA team leader, are you not?'

'I am.'

'Then it's always good to be perfectly clear on how to address your boss.' As she spoke the words, her mind jumped instantly to Leighton. He'd been her last boss, he'd also been her fiancé and neither of those things had ended well. She shook her head to clear the thoughts away. She was in a new place now, a new country, having a new experience. She didn't need to be dwelling on Leighton or her past.

He grinned at her words. 'Agreed.'

As they were now driving in the shade of the

trees, Melora lifted her glasses to the top of her head and glanced over at him. She found his smile to be so fresh, so encompassing it was causing a slight shift in the walls she'd built around herself. Just because Daniel Tarvon was tall, dark and extremely handsome, it didn't mean she couldn't appreciate it in a nice, friendly manner.

'So are you the type of person who likes everything to be neat and organised?' he asked.

'I used to be.'

'And now?'

'Now…who knows? My life has been jumbled up and turned inside out but where work is concerned, I confess I do like things to be clear. As a surgeon, when I operate, I prefer staff to ask me ten questions and get something right than to ask one question and get it wrong.'

'Surgery is all about absolutes,' he agreed.

'Are you a surgeon?'

'I'm a GP and a physician and a dentist and an obstetrician and a bit of an orthopaedist.'

'So I take it you get to see quite a variety out here?'

'Yes, and so will you.' He glanced over at her. 'I wonder if you know what you've really signed up for, Melora.'

She laughed but she was certain both of them heard the excited nervous tension. 'I've been wondering that myself ever since I stepped off the plane.'

'So what did prompt you to come to Tarparnii? I'm guessing it was the need to do something completely different, to recharge your love of medicine and to escape your own life for a spell.'

'How...how do you know that?' Had Emmy or Dart contacted him? Given him a precise of her situation?

He shrugged. 'It's a strange ability I've inherited from my mother, to sort of be able to see into people, to get a sort of sense from them.'

'Are you telling me you have psychic powers?' Melora looked at him in disbelief.

Daniel laughed, the sound washing over her with delight. 'Hardly. I leave that to Meeree. She's a woman who sees far more than you know and she's *always* right. In my case, though, it's more of a sense about someone. A gut feeling, I guess you could call it. I sometimes get...a feeling about someone or something. That's all.'

'Wow. I wish I had that ability. Would have saved me a lot of heartache.' She mumbled the last part, thinking that perhaps, if she'd had a smidgen of Daniel's ability, she might have realised that Leighton had been cheating on her.

'Sounds as though you've been through a bad time,' Daniel remarked, and it was only then she realised he'd heard her.

Not wanting to talk about it, she sat up straighter, holding on tighter to the side of the vehicle as he manoeuvred them out from the overhanging trees and back into the sunshine. 'That's all in the past. I'm here to have a new experience.'

'Ahh…the glass is half-full, eh?'

'Exactly.' She slipped her sunglasses back on and turned her face towards the sun, eager for the cobwebs to be removed from her life as she headed towards her new adventure.

They drove in silence for the next few minutes, back on a graded road that actually seemed to have more 'traffic', for want of a better word, travelling on it. There were several army-type trucks, most with big red crosses painted on them. There were bicycles, handcarts and other vehicles, just like theirs but in far worse condition, usually carrying far more than two or four passengers as had been the original car's design.

One car passed them with at least twenty people either sitting or hanging off the sides, the tyres almost flat from the weight. Everyone waved and called out greetings in the native Tarparniian guttural language. Daniel waved back, smiling brightly or beeping his horn jovially.

'Everyone seems so friendly,' Melora commented, mentally taking in everything around her. When they passed another such laden car, she found herself smiling and offering a very tentative wave.

'Not necessarily everyone,' Daniel remarked as they came around a corner to be faced with a barricade across the road. He slowed the Jeep and soon came to a complete stop. With the engine still running, he leaned over towards Melora and opened the glove-box, the flap of which flicked down and hit the tops of her knees.

'Sorry,' Daniel said, and before she knew what he was doing, he'd rubbed the tops of her knees where she'd been hit.

'It's fine.' She straightened her legs as best she could and scrunched herself as far away from him as possible. The warmth from his impromptu touch had filtered through the linen of her trousers, causing heat to spread from her knees up throughout her body. Thank goodness she hadn't worn a skirt today.

He found the papers he was looking for and closed the compartment, straightening as he did. When he turned to look at her, Melora felt for certain that she was blushing. 'Do you have your papers?' he asked.

'Pardon?' She was watching his mouth move but the words weren't sinking in due to the fact that she was still affected by the caring way he'd rubbed her knees. The action had been that of a parent, the touch, though, had definitely been one between a man and a woman. No colleague had ever penetrated her comfort zone so effortlessly, not even Leighton. Dr Daniel Tarvon, she was quickly coming to realise, really wasn't like any other man she'd ever met before.

'Your papers?' he asked again, and then pointed to the men who were standing next to the road-block. It was then that Melora realised what he was saying as the men had rifles slung over their shoulders and were checking the papers of all who wished to pass through the block.

'Oh! My papers.' She was pleased to focus on something other than trying to figure out just why Daniel seemed to be causing her mind to floun-der. Melora undid the piece of rope and climbed from the vehicle. Bending into the back seat to retrieve her bag, she rummaged around for her PMA papers. As she did so, she couldn't help but glance over at where Daniel was warmly shaking hands with the soldiers.

He knew them? Melora straightened, papers in hand, and looked over to where Daniel was laughing at something one of the soldiers had said. She felt highly self-conscious and completely out of her depth and for a moment the old Melora, the one who had needed to understand and have some semblance of control over every situation, returned.

What was she doing here? In this jungle country, with soldiers and guns and fighting going on somewhere near them? She tugged at the hem of her untucked shirt then checked that the collar and her scarf were still in place, keeping her well covered.

Just that morning she'd woken up in her apartment, had a shower, dressed, had finished packing her bag and caught a taxi to Sydney airport. It had still been dark, the sun not yet risen. She'd flown to Cairns where she'd switched planes to the small Cessna, which had flown her to Tarparnii. Then she'd climbed into a car with Daniel Tarvon and now was standing before men with guns. Daniel—a perfect stranger—was really the only person she knew.

It was all too…rudderless.

How had her world moved from knowing what she'd be doing every hour of every day of every week of every year to this? Standing at a check-point, about to hand over papers to a man with a rifle! When Emmy had suggested a complete change of scenery, she'd really meant a *complete* change.

For the past twenty months, Melora's life hadn't been her own due to the cancer that had attacked her body, but after lifesaving surgery, chemo-therapy and the return of her hair she was now determined to find the control that had been rudely taken from her with that first diagnosis.

She was different now. Not only mentally but physically as well. She'd made the decision to join PMA, she'd accepted this job here in Tarparnii, and now that new and, albeit, scary events were unfolding around her, she was determined to see them through.

She'd survived Leighton's betrayal. She'd sur-vived cancer. She could survive this!

Feeling a surge of determination and strength return, she straightened her shoulders, lifted her head high and headed over to where Daniel stood talking to the soldiers. With her smile pasted firmly in place, she held out her papers to the man Daniel was talking to…the man with the gun. 'Here you are.'

'Thank you.' The soldier spoke with an educated lilt to his tone, much the same as Daniel's.

'Melora, this is my second cousin, Paul.'

'Paul?' She was startled for a moment at such an English name. She put her smile back in place and nodded politely. 'Nice to meet you, Paul.' He checked over her papers and handed them back all neatly folded.

'Everything's in order,' Paul remarked. 'Have a great day.' He motioned to some of the other soldiers to lift the boom and as Melora and Daniel headed back to the Jeep, Paul called, 'Will I see you on Sunday at the bonfire?'

'Probably not. Depends on work,' Daniel replied, and gave his second cousin a high five as they drove past.

'Well, that was a little surreal,' Melora commented a few minutes later as they continued down the road.

'Going through a checkpoint? You'll get used to it. Just always make sure you have a set of papers with you. Usually the papers are for the vehicle, rather than just a single person, but as this was your first time, you needed to show your personal papers. Paul will make a record that you are officially in the country and working with PMA.'

'What happens if you don't have papers? Do they detain you? Hold you captive?' There was an edge of concern and disbelief in her voice.

'They detain you until someone can head back to the village, get the papers and bring them back to the checkpoint. Forgetting your papers usually results more in inconvenience rather than anything else.'

'Why did you need to show Paul your papers when he's your cousin? Surely he can vouch for who you are.'

'True, but, as I said, the papers are more for the vehicle logs than anything else. It's a strange system but it's a system that works.'

'It's so different.' Melora spoke softly and didn't think Daniel had heard her over the sound of the car's engine and the reverberation noise of the tyres on the graded road.

'That's what I thought the first time my father took me to England. So different.'

'You spent quite a bit of time there?' As he'd

opened the subject again, she didn't feel as though she was prying.

He nodded. 'I was educated there. Did my medical training there but always came back to Tarparnii for my holidays.'

'To spend time with your mother?'

'Exactly. She didn't like England that much so most of the time she preferred to stay here in Tarparnii with her village. My father was a doctor and one of the first to work here in Tarparnii. I was sent away to boarding school for many years.'

'You mentioned that you had sisters. Do they live here, too?'

'Yes they do. They're both married and so live in the villages of their husbands.'

'And your parents?' He really was quite a fascinating man. 'They're still together after all this time?'

'No. My father passed away six years ago.' The tone in his voice when he spoke of his father, however, was crisp and brisk, as it had been when he'd previously mentioned his father. It was clear the two had been at odds. 'My mother still lives in her village. She is the headwoman there and as such is needed to guide and care for her people.'

'Wow. I'm presuming being headwoman is important?'

His mouth creased into a smile. 'Very.'

'Do you see her often?'

'Quite often.' Daniel nodded. 'It depends on where I'm needed.'

'Work first?'

'Exactly.' He changed gear. 'Ready for a bit of cross-country?' This time, when he turned off, there didn't even appear to be tyre tracks on the ground.

'Do you know where you're going?' she couldn't help but ask as she held onto the windscreen with one hand and the bottom of her seat with the other as they bumped along the uneven terrain. This was very odd, very different, very…not normal.

Daniel laughed. 'This is my country, Melora. I know exactly where I am. This is my favourite short cut.'

'Short cut? Why…do…we need to take…a short cut?' The old car jolted up and down, jarring her words.

'Relax. Once we get through this area of dense forest, you'll have the most spectacular views.' There was a rumble from above them and she looked up to see clouds starting to gather, and quite quickly, too.

'Oh…well there's…no…need to go to…too… much trouble…for me…' she stumbled as she continued to bounce up and down in the Jeep. Her answer was more of Daniel Tarvon's easy laughter. 'Is…it going to…rain?' she asked.

Daniel glanced up. 'More than likely.'

'Do we…need some sort…of shelter? A roof…of sorts on the…car?' He didn't seem to be slowing down for any of the bumps.

'Why bother? It rains for about five minutes straight, we all get wet and then ten minutes after the rain has finished, we're all dry again. You'll get used to it.'

'I hope so.' She glanced over at him, at his strong profile. His nose was slightly crooked, indicating a break, and she idly wondered how it had happened. His unshaved chin and jawline were square and proud and she could tell by the smile on his lips that he was enjoying himself immensely. His large hands on the wheel were completely in control of the vehicle and his broad shoulders were strong and powerful as he continued to drive them through the dense forest.

When the rain came a few minutes later, the

heavens literally opening up to emit a torrential downpour, Melora told herself to relax, to enjoy, not to worry about every little thing. So she was getting soaked. That was OK. Daniel was getting soaked, too.

She'd spent so much of her life playing by the rules, doing what was right, following the guidelines set down by society at large, and she'd been incredibly successful at it. She'd been dux of her high school and medical school, had passed her general surgical training with full marks and was now a highly trained, highly competent surgeon.

But society at large had not prepared her for the upheaval cancer would bring into her world and now, having had enough of living by the rules, she was here, to have adventures such as driving in an old Jeep through a jungle while getting soaked.

The car swerved slightly to the side, the ground becoming more slick and slippery to drive on. Still Daniel didn't slow down and she knew that sometimes going faster over such ground was actually safer than slowing down.

They were almost at the top of the small mountain, the car's engine straining but not complaining as Daniel steered them ever onwards and upwards.

'How are you doing?' he called, glancing at her, his face, his hair, his body dripping with water. Melora blinked through the rain that had settled on her lashes, wanting to wipe her hand over her face, but was positive that her fingers had welded themselves to the sides of the Jeep in her effort to hold on.

'Good,' she called back, but no sooner had she spoken than a loud crack sounded behind them. 'What was that?'

'Uh…' Daniel gritted his teeth and put his foot down on the accelerator. 'You may want to hang on tight.'

'I *am* hanging on…tight.'

'Then hang on tighter,' Daniel remarked with a wild laugh as they crested the hill, the rain still pelting down on them. Another loud crack sounded and Melora's eyes widened. She hadn't seen any lightning in the sky so what on earth was making that noise? Another rumble and then the car started to slide again, Daniel instantly attempting to correct the direction of the tyres.

'Why? What's happening?' she called, but in the next instant the car lurched forward, and it had nothing to do with Daniel's driving.

He grinned at her, his brown eyes alive with the thrill of their situation.

'Daniel?' she called again as the car started to pick up speed. 'What is it?'

'Woo-hoo. *Mudslide!*'

CHAPTER TWO

'Wha?!'

There was panic in her tone, even though she was trying her hardest to stay calm. She'd wanted this, hadn't she? She'd wanted to step outside of her comfort zone, to step out of her normal life, to do something different. Well, this was different but a little *too* different. 'What?'

'Mudslide!' Daniel laughed again even as he concentrated on trying to control the steering-wheel as best he could. The rain was still pouring and they were heading down the hill at an even greater speed than Melora had expected…not that she'd expected, in her wildest dreams, to be trapped in a mudslide inside a car feeling more helpless than when she'd been diagnosed with cancer.

'Daniel!'

He glanced at her briefly, delight all over his face. 'Don't worry, Mel,' he called over the roar of nature around them. 'This happens all the time.

It's quite a tame one. Just hold on and enjoy the ride.'

'Tame?' The disbelief in her tone went unnoticed as Daniel continued to appear as though he did indeed have some sort of control over the vehicle. There was nothing left for her to do but trust him and hang on. Of one thing she was sure, her heart was pounding wildly against her chest with a surge of adrenalin. Exhilaration wasn't far behind and when the rain stopped, just as Daniel had said it would, she began to relax a little.

'I'm going to turn the wheel sharply and hope-fully disengage,' he called rapidly, Melora only hearing every second word. She was about to ask him to repeat himself when he yelled, 'Hang on!'

She tightened her grip, her knuckles white and wet, all feeling in her fingers having long since gone because she was holding on so hard. Then, with a quick full lock of the wheel and pressing down on the accelerator, the car jerked a sharp left and bumped its way over even rougher terrain than before.

'Ahh... Daniel! Watch out for that tree!' Melora yelled, but she needed not have worried as within another second Daniel had once again swerved before bringing the Jeep to a stop.

Neither of them moved for half a minute, Daniel being the first to recover. 'Whoo-ee. What a ride!' He undid his piece of rope-belt and stepped from the vehicle, his feet crunching down on leaves and twigs as he shook the rain from himself. She watched as he pulled his dark hair from its ponytail and pushed his fingers through the wet strands.

It gave him an even wilder look than before, like he really was a jungle man. The style didn't make him look at all feminine—in fact, it had quite the opposite effect. With his unshaven face, slightly crooked nose and his dark wet hair framing his face, he looked powerful, as though he could do anything, take on anything, such as navigating a car through a mudslide, and come out the winner.

She shook her head in wonderment as she watched him make his way around the front of the car to her side. She hadn't moved anything but her head, her arms still outstretched, her body still rigid, her heart thudding so loudly and powerfully throughout her body she was certain he could hear it.

'Are you all right?' he asked, coming to stand beside her.

'I...uh...' She swallowed and this time the powerful thudding of her heart had nothing at all to do with the roller-coaster slide they'd just finished but everything to do with the man before her. So strong, so virile, so masculine.

It was a shock for her to realise that she really was attracted to this man...to this man she barely knew but one who had probably just saved her life by his amazing ability to steer them through a mudslide. What woman in her right mind *wouldn't* be attracted to Daniel Tarvon? The fact that she wasn't at all in the market for any sort of romantic relationship was something she would do well to remember, but it was the way he was so easygoing, so relaxed, so personable that had made her instantly like him.

'Melora?' Daniel stepped closer and placed his hand over hers, gently prising her fingers from their clenched positions. 'Blood in the extremities?' He held her hands in his, rubbing his thumb and fingers over them, stimulating blood circulation. The intent was medical, the touch was personal.

She pulled her hands away from him and clenched them tightly together in her lap. 'It's fine. They're fine.' She fumbled with the piece of rope across her lap, which had indeed performed its job and kept her secure. 'I'm fine. Thank you,' she added, belatedly remembering her manners. She would be fine, would be able to get her heart rate back to a more normal and steady rhythm so long as Daniel kept his distance.

'Hop out and stretch your legs. Sorry about not being able to stop at the amazing view I'd previously promised but the mudslide obviously had different ideas.'

She laughed nervously, needing distance from him, and fast. 'I don't care much about the view right now. I'm just glad to be alive.' In more ways than one, she realised. It would have been ridiculous to have survived breast cancer only to be swept away down a hillside by a large mass of mud.

Melora carefully shifted her legs, making sure they were going to work before swivelling to the side and climbing from the vehicle, shaking her head politely at the hand Daniel stretched towards her to offer assistance. 'Thanks, but I'm fine.'

'As long as you really are and you're not just saying that so I'll leave you alone. The last thing I want to do is to deliver you to the village already in need of medical attention.'

She smiled, trying to control her reaction to

this man. Good looking, charismatic and funny. Definitely a lethal combination and one she had to confess she hadn't really expected to encounter here in Tarparnii.

'That would not be good.' Melora looked away from him as he pulled his hair back into a ponytail. She didn't need sexy visions of her new colleague penetrating her mind. She would need to put personal protocols in place to control her reaction to him. She was here to work, not flirt. She needed to remember that. Instead, she peered through the thin tree trunks around them. 'Exactly how far are we from the village?'

'It's about another ten minutes north-west of where we are now,' he replied as he started to inspect the car, making sure that it was still in working order.

'Oh. So not that far at all?' Melora decided to test her legs, to get them moving, and walked a little further away from the Jeep and away from Daniel Tarvon's powerful presence. 'Wait. Is that ten minutes by car or by walking?'

'Car.'

'Oh. Right.' She self-consciously pushed her hands through her short blonde hair, fluffing it out, surprised to find it already partially dry. She continued to pick her way through the fallen bark and bits of branches and leaves and goodness knew what else on the ground. The sounds of insects filled the air, birds flew high above them through the trees, water droplets hung from leaves and branches, the sun's rays peered through the clouds. It was definitely another world but it was an extremely beautiful world…and Daniel only enhanced it.

Having realised she was attracted to Daniel, she now found it difficult to look at him. It didn't matter that the attraction wouldn't—*couldn't*—go anywhere because at the moment her life wasn't technically her own. She still had to wait for results, results that would confirm or deny that she was cancer free. Who knew what sort of time bomb might be waiting to drop into her life? And to that end she was here to step outside her comfort zone and what she'd just come through—a mudslide in a Jeep—most definitely counted.

Something rustled in the bracken to her right and she stopped moving, peering closely, wondering if it was a pretty bird. 'Wait.' She peered further into the bushes, edging forward.

'Something wrong?' Daniel asked, standing up from where he'd been surveying the undercarriage of the car for damages. He brushed his hands to-gether as he headed in her direction.

'I don't know. I thought I saw something.' She peered through the branches and tree trunks, lis-tening carefully.

'What? Where?' Daniel was instantly by her side.

'Over there,' she pointed. 'I think I saw some-one.'

'What did you see?' His voice was calm but firm. 'Was it a group of men? There usually aren't soldiers in these parts of the forest because it's too densely populated.'

'Soldiers? No. It looked like one person. I think it was a woman or a girl. She was just over there. I promise you I'm not making this up.'

'I have no doubt you're telling the truth.' His gaze remained glued to the surrounding area.

'There!' She pointed. 'Daniel. Through there.' Melora pointed again and this time Daniel could see exactly where she meant.

There, in the scrub, were three women, all of them wet, one of them lying on the ground in pain. Daniel called out to them in his native language and Melora could see the two women who were trying to help their friend look around at him in fright. He said more words as they made their way towards them, the younger woman rushing forward to him.

'Dokta! *Qah*. Dokta.' She spoke in a rapid-fire way but Melora didn't need to hear what was going on. She could see it. The woman lying on the ground was in the last stages of labour, in the middle of a forest in the middle of nowhere.

'Melora.' Daniel turned to face her. 'Back in the car, down behind the back seat, is my medical bag,' he said.

'I'll get it,' she called needlessly, and hurried back to where he'd stopped the car. She found his medical bag but it was wedged beneath the seat. Grumbling when she realised she couldn't move the front seat forward to retrieve it, she climbed into the old Jeep and leaned over the seat, tugging the bag as best she could without causing any damage. Why was nothing ever simple?

Finally, she had the barely wet bag in her hands and headed back to where Daniel was now crouched down at the woman's feet, talking to her in calm, soothing tones.

'Here.' Melora put the bag down beside him and opened it up. She rummaged around for a second before pulling out gloves. 'Put these on.'

'Thanks.' He did so and on performing an examination found that the woman, who looked to
be about seventeen years old, was fully dilated.
'Contractions are only a few minutes apart.'

'What's her name?' Melora asked, and Daniel
turned and asked all their names.

The older woman was answering Daniel, the
stress and panic gone from her face now that the
'dokta' was here. Melora waited patiently for him
to translate.

'The mother is P'tanay, the young daughter is
K'hala and this brave woman...' he indicated the
woman in labour '...is J'tana.'

'A mother and her daughters?' The mother,
P'tanay barely looked old enough to have her
own children let alone about to be made a grandmother. K'hala, the other girl, looked to be about
thirteen. 'Isn't K'hala a little young to be witness-
ing a birth?' she asked quietly.

'No. K'hala would have seen many women
giving birth since she was very young. It's part
of the culture that young girls learn the ways of
women from the older women. Childbirth is an
important part of life for a Tarparniian woman
and it's an honour to be asked to assist. The only
men who are allowed around birthing women are

doctors and even then they prefer the doctors to be female.'

'Oh. Does that mean I need to take over?'

Daniel raised an eyebrow. 'Have you delivered many babies? I thought you were a general surgeon.'

'I am and...uh...I delivered a few during my internship.'

'Many years ago, no doubt. Well, consider this birth a refresher course, Melora, because you're bound to see a few more during your time in Tarparnii. Today you can be my assistant.' He smiled up at her and Melora felt the full effect of his handsome face, his bright twinkling brown eyes, his perfectly straight teeth and his slightly crooked nose. Sunlight was shining down through the trees onto his dark hair, almost giving him a halo effect. Daniel Tarvon? A saint? Well, she was sure these three women thought him so.

Melora swallowed and forced herself to look away from the man before her, forced her mind to concentrate so she could be of assistance to him rather than an imbecile who stood there ogling him. So he was handsome. That didn't mean a thing. She'd dated handsome doctors before, she'd even been engaged to a handsome doctor, but her life had changed and she was no longer the woman she'd once been. End of story.

Pushing that thought and all others from her mind, she put on her game face. 'OK, *boss*. What do you need me to do?'

'While we're waiting for the baby's head to crown, which should happen any time within the next few contractions, I need you to find something to wrap the baby in. While it's quite warm today, we need to keep the baby as warm as possible.'

'Right. I'll check the Jeep.' But even as she headed back to the vehicle, she knew exactly what she'd find in the back seats. Her bag. As she circled around the car, she noted the spare tyre, a jerrycan full of petrol and another full of water locked into the very rear of the Jeep. She managed to unlock the jerrycan with h2o written in bright letters on the outside and put it on the ground. Next, she unzipped her large bag and began rummaging for something they could use to wrap the baby in after its birth.

She'd been told by PMA that all bedding would be provided but she'd still packed her own things. She'd packed two travel towels so pulled out one to use now. She found a large cotton shirt she used for painting, which she could tear up if necessary.

Next, she pulled free her very compact sleeping bag, which would be perfect for keeping the baby warm.

Where she ordinarily liked her things to be packed neatly and tidily, she gritted her teeth, shoved everything back into her bag and zipped it closed. Now was not the time for fastidiousness but rather for helping out in an emergency. Gathering her things and the jerrycan of water, she headed back to Daniel and the women.

'Ah, good. You found the water,' he said. 'I had meant to ask you to bring it down. Well done, Melora. We'll make a jungle doctor out of you yet.'

'Thanks.' She tried not to show how pleased she was at his praise. She was a surgeon, she was out of her depth and she hadn't been praised by a peer in years, and yet it still felt wonderful to hear those words. While she appreciated the seriousness of what they were doing, knowing that anything could go wrong at any given moment, she couldn't ignore the fact that she was also excited about being able to help out at such a special time. She guessed that jungle doctors needed to practise jungle medicine!

She showed Daniel the other things she'd brought

down to assist with the delivery as they sat on the ground at J'tana's feet. P'tanay and K'hala were muttering soothing words, helping J'tana through this difficult time.

'Great. We'll wrap the baby in the towel and keep it warm with the sleeping bag.' J'tana moaned again, gritting her teeth against the pain, trying not to call out, and Daniel checked the status of the baby. 'Head is definitely crowning.' He spoke in Tarparnese and even though Melora couldn't understand him, she could see through his expression and hear in his tone that his words were of encouragement.

Melora took another look through Daniel's medical bag and noticed he'd already used the stethoscope as it was lying on top of other things. Below it, she saw a portable sphygmomanometer. She pulled both out and once the contraction had finished, she shifted around with her equipment, getting into position to do the observations.

'Thanks, Mel. I was just about to suggest you check her blood pressure for me.' He rapidly explained to the women what she was going to do and they moved aside so Melora could do her job.

'Blood pressure is slightly elevated but within normal range,' she reported as she hooked the stethoscope into her ears and pressed it first to J'tana's heart and then to her abdomen. 'All within normal range,' she announced.

'Good. Thanks. While this is J'tana's first baby, it's coming quickly, although her mother did say that J'tana had been in labour on and off for the past few days.'

'Poor girl.'

'They thought they'd be able to make it to the clinic but apparently the baby was impatient to make its entrance into the world.'

'They were almost there, almost made it to the village. What strong, brave women they are.' Melora smiled at all three of them and P'tanay smiled back. She said something to Daniel and he quickly translated.

'She says thank you.'

'She can understand me?'

'She said she's heard the English phrase "strong, brave women" before and she thanks you for thinking it of her and her daughters.' Daniel's smile increased. 'Looks as though you've made your first new friends in Tarparnii.'

This news made Melora feel incredible.

It made her realise that out here it didn't matter what degrees she held or what research projects she'd undertaken. Careers were important within hospital walls, not in the jungle. Out here, she was a doctor who had come to help and the Tarparniian people were extremely grateful for that help.

J'tana gritted her teeth and pushed again, and with this contraction the baby's head came out completely. As they waited for the shoulders to rotate, Melora once more did the observations and then started to prepare for the next stage of labour. She found locking forceps, ready to clamp the cord, scissors for cutting the cord and a small container she could use to put water into.

As she continued to get set up, Melora watched the way Daniel was interacting with his patient. He was all ease and friendliness. There was no falseness about him and again she compared him to the crisp, by-the-book surgeons she'd been working with for the past few years.

She compared him to some of the doctors she'd had during her mastectomy surgery and while they had been top in their field, Melora had quickly realised that bedside manner did indeed count a lot towards a patient's level of recovery. Daniel Tarvon seemed to have an amazing bedside manner and her opinion of him increased.

'Shoulders have rotated,' he announced. 'Just a

few more good pushes, J'tana.' He said the words in English but then broke into Tarparnese half-way through. The young mother didn't cry out but gritted her teeth and pushed as hard as she could, sweat on her brow, breath held, pain in her eyes. This was hard labour.

Soon Daniel was lifting the healthy-sized baby boy and Melora held out her towel, accepting the child. She wrapped him loosely, rubbing his little body, stimulating him to breathe while cleaning off the vernix. She could feel the cord pulsating and silently counted the beats, watching his chest for any sign of movement.

'He's bradycardic. We have to get him breathing.' She looked around, feeling helpless without any sort of medical equipment. 'We need suction and oxygen, Daniel. What do I do?' There was veiled panic in her tone.

'Relax, Melora. All you need to do is put your mouth over his mouth and nose and suck any obstruction out of the way. That should do the trick.'

'What?' Disbelief was written all over her face. Was he joking or serious?

'That's all you need to do. It'll work. Trust me.'

Trust him? She'd known him for less than an

hour! Well…what else was she supposed to do? The baby wasn't breathing.

'Here goes,' she mumbled quietly to herself, and did as Daniel had suggested. Thankfully it worked and within another few seconds the baby gurgled, his little face contorted and he gave a hoarse cry.

Everyone exhaled. J'tana smiled and collapsed back into the bracken, her eyes closed, fatigue starting to wash over her. The baby was OK.

Daniel stripped the cord as best he could with his fingers before reaching for the locking forceps and the scissors. He clamped and cut the cord and Melora re-wrapped the crying baby boy, ensuring he was dry and warm.

J'tana accepted the baby with pride, mother and sister speaking and cooing rapidly at the baby, showering him with love. Melora smiled, surprised to find tears misting her eyes at the sight.

'Gets to me every time, too,' Daniel murmured, and when she looked at him she realised he mirrored the look of wonderment that no doubt was on her own face. The miracle of life, the amazing healthy delivery of a perfectly formed human being. The world was indeed an awesome place. 'We just need to deliver the placenta and then we can get everyone into the Jeep and head for the village.'

'What do you usually do with the placenta? I mean, we're out in the middle of nowhere and I don't have anything you can put it in. Do you bury it?'

'Can't. *Ha'kuna* will dig it up and eat it. That gives them a taste for human flesh.' Daniel looked around them at their surroundings then pointed. 'Over there. See those large dry leaves from the trees.' Melora nodded, the trees looking a lot like banana trees with long, wide leaves. Daniel continued. 'Gather a few of those and we'll wrap the placenta in that, take it back to the village and burn it.'

'It really is a different world,' she muttered as she went to do as she was told. Once the placenta had been delivered, Daniel checked it then wrapped it as securely as he could with the leaves. While he was doing that, Melora used the shirt strips and water, mixed with disinfectant, to help cleanse J'tana.

When next she looked at the mother, she had the young babe to her breast, the child suckling hungrily. Melora swallowed, the natural sight bringing an instant pain to her heart. It was what breasts were meant for, to feed and nourish a child.

For her, though, that wasn't the case.

One whole breast had been removed, as well as the cancerous lymph nodes. Part of her body, a vital part that expressed her femininity, had been cut from her in order to save her life. She knew she was fortunate, she knew that her prognosis was considered favourable, and she really couldn't ask for more than that.

She knew she was privileged to live in a time where treatments such as radiotherapy and chemotherapy could assist in keeping patients cancer free for the rest of their lives and she desperately wanted that to be the case. The fact that she'd left it too late to have children, to nuzzle a baby to her breast, just like J'tana, was something she would have to live with. She'd concentrated on her career, pushing the thought of marriage and children into the 'later' box. Now, though, that box was out of reach and she envied J'tana the natural ability to breastfeed her child.

'Melora?'

At the sound of her name, she turned quickly to look at Daniel, unaware there were tears streaming silently down her cheeks until it was too late. He'd already seen.

'Melora? What is it?' he asked quietly. 'What's wrong?'

Melora bit her lip and shook her head, breaking her gaze away from his expressive brown eyes, which were filled with concern. He watched as she continued to roll up the strips of her shirt she'd been using to help cleanse J'tana, tidying things up and then pulling off her gloves, tying them into an enclosed ball.

She brushed a hand across her face and concentrated on controlling her breathing. Daniel wasn't at all sure what had just happened but the look he'd seen on her face had been one of utter desolation. He knew people came to Tarparnii for many different reasons. Some wanted a break from their lives, some were running away from something, some simply wanted to forget.

He'd learned that it didn't really matter why these professionals came to help, just that they *came*. The people and the lifestyle in Tarparnii had helped many of his friends in the past and as he'd witnessed the pain on Melora's face as she'd watched J'tana feed the baby, he hoped Tarparnii would have the same healing effect on her as it had had on others.

As they continued to pack everything away, Melora having taken J'tana's blood pressure again and listened to the baby's heartbeat, pronouncing herself satisfied, Daniel assisted the new mother into the Jeep. J'tana was positioned in the back seat, lying as best she could, leaning up against her sister. Melora had insisted P'tanay sit in the front but the new grandmother had declined and squeezed into the back with her daughters.

Sitting in the front seat, with her large bag on her lap, which almost obscured her vision, was how Melora finally arrived in the village. Daniel beeped the horn as they drove up and soon they were surrounded by several people, all coming out to see what the ruckus was about. When they realised what had happened, J'tana and her baby were whisked away, the rest of her family following.

'Welcome to our village.' The greeting came from a small but slim Tarparnii woman with grey hair, wise eyes and a heartfelt smile. 'I am Meeree and this is my husband, Jalak. He is the headman of the village.' Meeree held both of Melora's hands in hers, turning them in a small circle, as was the customary Tarparniian greeting.

'Thank you. I am very honoured to be here.' Melora smiled politely, greeting Jalak as well. 'Your country, what I've seen of it so far, is beautiful and…energetic.' She added the last word as she recalled the mudslide adventure she'd experienced. She looked over her shoulder, expecting to see Daniel close by, but was surprised to find he'd disappeared.

'He has gone to take care of other matters,' Meeree said, and it was then Melora remembered the placenta. Daniel was obviously doing what needed to be done.

'Of course. Yes.'

'Please. You will come and have something to drink. You must wash and become refreshed.' Meeree put her arm through Melora's and started leading the way. Melora quickly bent to pick up her bag but found that Jalak, a man she gauged to be in his late seventies but still appearing very sprightly, had hefted it up onto his shoulder and was carrying it with ease.

As she walked further into the village, Melora was charmed by what she saw. There were quite a number of bamboo huts with woven leaves for screens and walls and all had cone-shaped thatched roofs. The huts were raised from the ground and in many places there were slatted walkways that joined the huts together. This was obviously to keep them above the mud that would no doubt gather in the wetter months but for now everything was quite dry.

Many of the huts also had little gardens out in front, filled with native flora, the bright flowers and non-deciduous bushes bright with a mix of colours. There were also gardens devoted solely to specific vegetables and Melora knew that some-where else would be even bigger areas of food production.

There were chickens, a few ducks and some goats roaming about the place, mixing in with the pleth-ora of children who seemed to be running about, chasing each other, laughing, clapping and having a good time. There was a large fire area where a lot of their food would be cooked, and also a well, both situated near the centre of the clearing for all to use.

Some women were crouched on the ground, using a crude form of mortar and pestle to grind things; others were mixing and some were knead-ing a large doughy mass on a flat bamboo-style mat, their guttural language surrounding them as they talked.

'What a wonderful community you have here,' she found herself saying as she stood next to Meeree and drank it all in. 'It's so vibrant and alive.'

'I thank you most humbly,' Meeree remarked, waiting patiently for Melora to finish looking at the new sights before her. When Melora was ready, she was welcomed into Meeree and Jalak's hut, thankful to pour some water into a basin and wash her hands, face and arms. What she really wanted was a hot shower but knew that wasn't on the cards for the next two weeks. She'd done her research. She knew what to expect.

Except for Daniel Tarvon, a quiet voice inside her head remarked, and she realised it was true. She hadn't expected to like what she'd seen in him, and where she'd initially been wary, the way he'd handled the vehicle during the mudslide, the way he'd kept them both safe, had definitely made her drive from the airport to the village a bonding experience. Add to all of that the shared assistance in delivering a child, working together in the face of an emergency, needing to trust each other instantly in a medical capacity...yes, Melora had come to trust him in a personal sense as well.

Even after she'd had a drink and eaten some

delightful exotic fruits, one which tasted like a cross between a pear and a banana, she couldn't help but wonder where Daniel had disappeared to. Was he checking on J'tana? Should she go, too? Was there something else happening? Something medical? Did he require her services somewhere?

'He is seeing to his duties,' Meeree said softly, standing and walking to her front door. Melora wasn't sure what the other woman was talking about at first but when Meeree motioned for her to follow, Melora headed outside to stand on the top step, looking out into the village clearing.

There she saw Daniel, surrounded by several children, laughing and enjoying a joke with them, but there was one little girl, with big brown eyes and little blonde pigtails, who was held securely and protectively in his arms.

'His duties?' She found herself asking, unable to take her eyes from him.

'It is the duty of a parent to greet their family when returning to the village. Daniel Tarvon is greeting his daughter, Simone.'

'His *daughter*?' Melora asked with incredulity, her eyes wide with surprise as she took in the sight of father and daughter.

CHAPTER THREE

HE WAS a father?

As she looked across at him, holding his daughter, laughing and kissing her sweet skin, Melora's heart softened. It looked so natural—father and daughter—and it was evident that he loved her a great deal.

The hollow pit inside her, the one she'd vowed not to think about, started to make itself known. She had been looking forward to starting a family with Leighton, to finally becoming a mother, and now that part of her life was definitely over. She knew it was almost impossible that she would one day feel the same parental love that she could see written on Daniel's face. He was, most definitely, a lucky man.

She could feel Meeree studying her and it was then she remembered Daniel saying that Meeree was a woman of insights. Even though they'd only just met, did Meeree have insights into her? Could the woman see the pain and anguish that had previously made up Melora's life? It made her feel self-conscious and she tugged at the hem of her shirt and then checked the top buttons were still securely in place, her fingers fussing with the edges of the scarf around her neck.

She had come here to Tarparnii to search out a newness that her life had been missing. Too much had gone wrong and where she'd wallowed, feeling as though she'd been walking through the season of winter, her life bleak and hopeless around her, once her chemotherapy had ended she'd decided that enough had been enough.

Tarparnii and the experience she would have here offered her hope. Already today she'd been on a scary but exhilarating mudslide ride, had assisted with the birth of a newborn babe and made friends with the locals. While the opportunity to have children may have passed her by, she'd been blessed in other ways, and finding the silver lining in her situation was what she was trying her hardest to do. She watched as Daniel tickled his daughter, the child's laughter ringing out across the village.

'He's a lucky man,' she murmured.

'He would say he makes his own luck but, yes, he has been most fortunate in having such a wonderful child,' Meeree remarked. 'He is a caring father. That is who Daniel is. He is always bright and smiling, caring for everyone, but his heart has known great sadness and the child in his arms brings him comfort.'

She was thoughtful as the woman's words floated around her. 'His wife has passed away?'

'Yes. She died. They were not here but back in the other country belonging to Daniel. B'lana, his *par'machkai*—his wife—was ill. She was a woman raised in two countries, this one and another one, like Daniel. When her sickness became too much, he took her there for stronger medicines but they would harm the babe. B'lana said no. The babe must remain strong and now look at the child today. Simone is bright and strong, as was the wish of her mother.'

'It can't be easy for Daniel to raise her on his own.' Her admiration for the man increased yet again.

'Not on his own. She is here.' Meeree spread her arms wide. 'With a large family who love her. Every child here belongs to the village and the village belongs to them.'

Melora instantly smiled. 'That's so great for the children.'

'You do not have a large family?'

'No.' She looked away from Daniel and his daughter. 'I'm an only child and one who generally prefers the company of a good book to the company of others, but I'm trying to change.'

'Coming here is something new for you.'

Melora laughed. 'Yes, exactly.'

'Then I am glad you are here.' With a brief touch of warm welcome on her arm, Meeree smiled before turning away and heading over to where a young child of about two had fallen over and was crying.

Melora returned her attention to where Daniel and his daughter had been playing and was almost startled to find him standing before her, his gorgeous little girl still firmly in his arms, her hands wrapped lovingly around his neck.

'Melora, this is my daughter, Simone.' At his words, Simone smiled.

'I'm four and three-quarters, nearly five,' she said with a perfect English accent.

'Wow. You certainly look very much like an almost-five-year-old,' Melora remarked, smiling at the child.

'How old you are?' Simone wanted to know.

Daniel grimaced. 'Simone. You know it's not polite to ask grown-ups their age.' He gave Melora an embarrassed smile. 'Sorry. Lately she's become highly fascinated with everyone's ages.'

'It's all right. I don't mind.' Melora met the little girl's gaze directly. 'I'm forty-one.'

'So is my daddy!' Simone sat up straighter in his arms and unwound her hands from his neck, clapping them with delight. 'You're the same.'

'It appears we are,' Melora agreed with a bright smile.

'And *we* are the same.' Simone pointed between the two of them and then touched her blonde pigtails. 'We have yellow hair but mine is lots longer. Nobody else has yellow hair in the village. They all have black.' The child tipped her head to the side and raised a finger to her chin as though she was thinking. 'Emmy has red hair but she's not here now and Gloria has lots of different colours but she's not here now, too.'

'All right,' Daniel interjected. 'Enough about hair colours, *Separ.* We need to show Melora around the village.'

'Sounds good.' Melora nodded, already half in love with the gorgeous four-year-old.

'This way.' When he inclined his head, she descended the few steps to the ground and followed him. 'How's the acclimatisation process going?'

'It's a lot to take in,' she remarked. 'This world is so different from my own, especially the notification and charting of age and hair colour.' She smiled at Simone.

Daniel chuckled. 'Especially *that*.' He shifted Simone to his other hip, grumbling about how big his daughter was getting. The little girl giggled and it was clear that the two of them were very close. A father having a close relationship with his daughter. It was so nice to see, especially as Daniel had already mentioned that he hadn't connected with his own father.

'Quick layout, just so you can get your bearings. Over here,' he said, pointing, 'are the huts the PMA staff share. They're all quite full at the moment so we're not exactly sure where you'll be sleeping.'

'Oh.'

'Don't stress. We'll find room.' He smiled reassuringly at her and Melora found herself responding with a small smile of her own.

'Thank you.'

'That hut at the end,' he continued, 'is the food hut so if you're hungry at any time, head in there and you'll be able to find something to eat and drink. Cold meats, fruits, breads, that sort of thing. And over here is the brilliant and wonderful medical clinic. Only two years old and still very precious.' Daniel walked over and stroked the mud-brick building, making Melora laugh.

'Ah, yes. Emmy has told me about the clinics. I hear they have running water.'

'Such a luxury,' he confirmed with a nod. 'It was Emmy and Dart who commissioned them and while it may have taken a while to actually have them built, we're all forever grateful. We have four clinic rooms, two treatment rooms and a small six-bed area that serves as a recovery and general ward.'

He put a jiggling Simone down and within seconds she'd run off to join her friends, her blonde hair making her easily stand out amongst the rest of the children.

'Do I stand out that much?' Melora absentmindedly touched her short, blonde hair.

'Yes.' The one word was soft and quickly spoken and when she turned to look at him, it was to find him regarding her with an intense expression. 'But that's not necessarily a bad thing.'

Their gazes held for a long moment and she felt as though Daniel had just reached out and caressed her cheek. It was the oddest sensation. Melora dropped her hand back to her side and swallowed, desperate to ignore the frisson of awareness that seemed to spring up between them.

'Uh…how are J'tana and the baby?' She glanced at the building behind them, thankfully breaking the contact. Now all she had to do was to ignore the residual tingles that were still flowing through her body. Had Daniel Tarvon just implied she was beautiful? If only he knew the truth about her. No. She wasn't beautiful.

'Both doing very well.' He gestured that they should go inside and again she found herself following him.

'When will they start to head back to their own village?'

'Not for a few more days, possibly a week. It depends how long it takes J'tana to feel up to walking all that way again.'

'Can't they be driven back in a car?'

Daniel shook his head. 'Only to a certain point, and we'd have to go through about five checkpoints to get there. Some villages don't have access by any roads. There are places here that are more easily accessed on foot. That's one of the reasons why we do clinics in different places, the larger villages or ones with other smaller communities around them, to provide easier access for more people.'

'Fair enough.' Talking about their patient and shifting the conversation back to a medical-related focus had helped Melora to feel more calm, more in control, rather than being aware of the man beside her.

Inside the clinic, Daniel pointed things out and even turned on the taps for her. 'I know you probably think it's next to nothing, given that back in Australia you can turn on taps without thinking about where the water's coming from, but here—it really is like a miracle.'

'Daniel. I understand,' she said with a smile. 'You don't have to explain. I think it's brilliant that there's running water and that it makes you feel like a child in a candy store at Christmastime.'

He returned her smile. 'Yes. Yes, it does.' As they stood there in the small examination area, he couldn't help but admire how Melora seemed to be taking everything in. Over the years, he'd seen numerous people come here to help and take weeks, if not months to settle in. Some *never* settled in but apparently Melora Washington wasn't one of them.

While it was clear she was out of her comfort

zone, Daniel had the sense that it didn't have all that much to do with being in a completely foreign environment. Something had made her cry as she'd stood and watched J'tana feed her newborn baby. Whatever had caused that reaction was no doubt the real reason why Melora had seemed upset.

As they went through to check on J'tana, he decided to hang back a little, watch how she handled the situation, but as soon as P'tanay saw her, she rushed over and, speaking rapidly, touched Melora's blonde hair.

Melora smiled, feeling highly self-conscious at being touched. She looked to him for a translation and he nodded.

'You're quite right, P'tanay,' he said in Tarparnese, before looking at Melora. 'She says that with thanks to the "bright" woman who was there for the delivery of her first grandson, they're going to name the baby J'torek, which means child the bright light shines on, or child of good fortune.'

'My hair?' She looked astounded, pleased and almost fit to bursting with excitement. 'They're naming the baby after my hair?'

'Yes.' Daniel stepped closer. 'It's better than them naming him after your nose.' He winked at her and she felt a thrill of delight pass through her. It was odd how a bit of teasing, a bit of joking around with her new colleague could give her such a feeling, but as she usually worked with up-tight, stiff doctors back in Sydney, his words had been refreshing.

'What's wrong with my nose?' she asked quietly, a glint of appreciation in her eyes.

His grin increased. 'Nothing. However, your hair, now, that is really something. People here are fascinated by it. P'tanay says that the "bright" woman brought good fortune on her daughter, that it was you who saw them, you who helped with the delivery and that is why you should have the honour.'

Melora was almost fit to bursting with pride. 'Me? I am touched. I'm so grateful.' She said the words to P'tanay. 'Oh, Daniel. Will you please translate that for me? Please?'

Melora's excitement was highly contagious and Daniel translated her words, watching as she clutched her hands lovingly to her chest as though she was accepting an imaginary award. And in some ways she was…accepting the award of having a child named after her.

'I'm touched. I'm so…well…apparently I'm speechless.' Melora turned to the mother and bowed a little. 'Thank you,' she said. Daniel translated her words and then, to her surprise, P'tanay embraced her. Melora was momentarily stunned but carefully returned the embrace, patting the grandmother on the shoulder. P'tanay drew back, talking and smiling and touching Melora's hair one last time.

'Congratulations, Melora,' Daniel remarked placing his arm around her shoulders and drawing her close. The instant he touched her he realised he might have made a mistake as her entire body tensed. He quickly broke the contact and stepped back. It had been a natural reaction to embrace her as that was simply how the staff here reacted to good news.

Sharing the highs and lows of this job could only really be done by those who were in the thick of it with you. As such, the friendships formed between staff usually became very strong. They would often link arms when walking, or they'd hug—either for comfort and support or for encouragement or even for celebration. Platonic physical contact was very high between the staff members.

Daniel was curious to observe Melora's reaction to her other colleagues. The big question was *why* didn't she like being touched? What had happened to her in her past to make her withdrawn? Perhaps her childhood hadn't been all that happy? Maybe her parents hadn't been the demonstrative type? His own father had been cold and sometimes rejecting, especially when it had come down to showing vulnerable emotions. His mother, on the other hand, was warm and inviting and always had been.

Melora insisted on taking J'tana's blood pressure and listening to her heartbeat, pronouncing herself satisfied that the readings were all within normal limits. He also watched as she checked the baby, listening to his chest and checking the range of movement of his legs and arms. J'torek looked robust and healthy but was starting to make his impatience known at being poked and prodded by the 'bright' doctor.

'He's going to get stroppy with you in a minute, Melora,' Daniel remarked good-naturedly.

She laughed and the soft tinkling sound washed over him, warming him through. He stopped at that thought, watching as she swaddled the babe once more and gave him a little cuddle. Her laughter had warmed him. That was odd because the last woman who had evoked such a reaction had been B'lana, his wife.

Daniel shook his head, as though to clear it, realising he must have imagined the sensation. B'lana's death had left a large hole in his life, one that had taken almost four years to patch over. He wasn't sure the area was strong enough for him to mentally walk on and, besides, he wasn't sure he wanted to. Naturally, he found Melora attractive, but there wasn't a red-blooded male who wouldn't.

She was about five feet eight inches, had honey-brown eyes which he'd already realised were highly expressive whether she was excited, scared or simply happy. Her cheekbones were defined, her nose was straight and her lips were a natural plump pink…the kind of lips that were perfect for kissing.

'Whoa!' The word sprang from his lips.

'Something wrong, Daniel?' Melora asked as she held little J'torek while his mother found a position comfortable enough to be able to feed the baby once more.

Daniel quickly cleared his throat, reminding himself he had no need to be embarrassed because Melora couldn't read his thoughts—thankfully. 'No. Fine. Carry on.'

What was wrong with him? What had he been

thinking? He must surely be insane to be actually wondering what Melora's lush pink lips would taste like! It was definitely out of the ordinary for his thoughts to head in that direction, especially about a colleague. Being friends and keeping relationships happy and amicable was part of his job as PMA team leader so he definitely had no business thinking about those plump lips of hers.

He also had other things, more private things, on the boil in the back of his mind, and top of the list was Simone. Now that she was getting closer to the age where she should be attending school, he had some big decisions to make. Having been given every opportunity by living in two very different countries, even if he'd garnered a lot of resentment back then, Daniel knew the importance of a good education.

However, he couldn't bring himself to 'post' Simone off to boarding school and then leave her like a forgotten letter—just as he had been. He wasn't barbaric like his own father and was determined to be a major part of his daughter's life.

J'torek started to cry, bringing Daniel's thoughts back to the present. He watched as Melora cuddled him close before pressing a kiss to his head and handing him back to his mother. 'I think he's getting mighty impatient.' She looked at J'tana, touching her bunched fingers to her mouth, indicating food. 'He's a very healthy boy.' She put two thumbs up to show her approval but Daniel quickly translated her words for her.

J'tana smiled tiredly and settled down to feed her child. Melora felt that same tightening of her insides at watching woman and child, in the way they'd been designed for each other. It was good. It was right, and the fact that it wouldn't happen to her was completely beside the point. She was happy for J'tana and clenched her jaw, ignoring the hollowness that once more rose within her.

Feeling as though the walls were starting to close in on her, Melora smiled politely at the three women before excusing herself and heading out into the fresh air. Once there, she dragged in a few deep breaths, focusing her thoughts on the positives in her life. She had good, supportive friends and an exciting adventure ahead of her.

She heard a sound behind her and quickly looked over her shoulder, not surprised to see Daniel standing there.

'Everything all right?' he asked as he walked to her side. She looked at him, nodded and smiled.

'I'm fine. It's just wonderful to have a happy

ending for J'tana and her new son. He has a good set of lungs on him, that's for sure.'

Daniel nodded but looked at her closely. Melora wondered what it was he could see and just as she was starting to squirm inside, he took a step to the side and beckoned her closer. 'Come with me.' He indicated a well-worn path that led away from the village. 'There's something I'd like to show you.'

'Oh. OK.' Once more, Melora found herself following him, trusting this man she really didn't know all that well, but as he was the person she knew *most* in this country, she did as he asked.

Without a word, they walked along the path. It was fairly open, not surrounded by dense scrub but with enough foliage that Daniel had to hold back a few bushes for her to pass by. Neither of them wore a hat, nor did they wear sunglasses, but thankfully the sun wasn't too hot. She swatted at an insect as they headed along, looking around her and drinking in the very different scenery to the city buildings she was used to.

In the past, she'd been quite content with her life. She'd studied hard, worked hard, built her career and attained the position as a general surgical consultant. She'd found a man she'd wanted to spend the rest of her life with, had become engaged and planned to live happily ever after.

She shook her head. That wasn't how life happened. It wasn't how things had turned out and during the past two years she'd changed into a woman who'd been desperate to find a way to gain some control over her life. Out here, in this lovely scenery, she felt the tension and stress that had plagued her begin to ebb. She imagined herself sitting out here with her sketchpad or, if time permitted, her water-colours. The problem, she soon realised, was choosing which glorious landscape to capture. She was spoiled for choice.

They continued on and within another few minutes Daniel left the path and beckoned her over. 'Come take a look at this,' he encouraged.

Melora followed him and then gasped as they came to a thick, large tree trunk, but the tree had been split in two, the trunk wide open. The detail in the bark, the gnarly twists of the knots, the thickness of the roots—it was utterly exquisite. 'Lightning?'

'Yes. Well over twenty years ago now but this tree always reminds me that out of bad things, good things can grow.' He pointed to the new growth, the small tree that was growing right in the middle of the split trunk. The original tree still had foliage on it, its roots sunk deep into the ground.

'My wife died,' he ventured, hoping that if he opened up to her a little, just a little, she'd open up to him. He wasn't asking for massive revelations but something was obviously bothering her and as PMA team leader, he wanted to help. Telling her a bit about B'lana might help her to trust him a little more. It was definitely worth a shot.

'Meeree mentioned it.'

Daniel didn't seem annoyed at Meeree having told her. 'B'lana was like me. Raised in two different countries but where my father was British, her father was Tarparniian and insisted that his daughter be raised in the ways of her country. She was Tarparniian first, British second, whereas for me, my father made sure it was the other way around.' Daniel reached out and stroked a hand down the tree, the tactile sensation providing importance, providing physical connection.

'This tree has always held such significance for me. I often felt as though I was split in two, raised loving two different cultures.'

'And your life here with your daughter is that the new little tree, that new growth growing right in the middle?'

Daniel's smile at the mention of his daughter was automatic. 'Yes.' He paused. 'When B'lana died, I felt as though I'd been struck by lightning again, that my life had been ripped open and I was exposed…raw.'

Melora nodded, knowing that sort of sensation all too well. She felt as though she'd been struck by lightning, that her life had been ripped apart by forces beyond her control.

'I don't want to pry, Melora, but out here, working in such a small community and in an often stressful environment, it's paramount that we're able to keep ourselves focused. Seeing J'tana with her baby affected you deeply. Over fifty per cent of our patients are pregnant women, some younger than J'tana, some in their forties having their tenth or eleventh child. On a strictly work-related basis, I need to know that you're going to be able to handle seeing them with their children.'

Anger and heat started to rise within Melora and she clenched her teeth together. 'I'm a professional, Dr Tarvon. I'll do my job.'

'I'm not saying that you won't.' He hadn't missed the way she'd called him by his title and surname. He'd angered her with his words, not what he'd meant to do. He simply wanted her to open up a little so he knew how best to guide her while she was there. 'What I am saying is that I get the feeling that your life has been split in two, just like this tree. I don't know what might have happened to you but I have the feeling that it has something to do with babies.'

She straightened her shoulders, pushing aside the emotions of her heart and pulling on her professionalism. 'No. Not babies, per se.' Slowly, she met her new colleague's gaze. 'I don't think my past, whether my life has been split in two or not, is of any relevance at the moment.'

'It is if it affects your work,' he countered.

'It won't.'

'You can't know that for sure, Melora.'

'I can. I've been a highly competent, fully qualified general surgeon for quite a number of years. Medicine has been my main focus for over half my life and learning to control my own personal feelings has been part of that training, as I'm sure you well understand.'

'But out here, out in the middle of a jungle…' Daniel spread his arms wide, indicating the fact that they really were, for all intents and purposes, standing in the middle of nowhere '…emotions have a way of sneaking up on you and slapping you fair in the face.

'You've come here for a change, Melora, and for that alone I applaud you. However, the majority of people who come to provide medical aid in Tarparnii are usually trying to escape from something. It might be that they need to recharge their batteries, to remember why they decided to pursue medicine in the first place, or it might be because their ordinary life has dealt them a cruel blow and they feel so at odds with their life that they simply want to run away.'

He raked both hands through his hair, needing to get through to her. 'Dart, Emmy's husband, came here regularly for six years before he was even able to face the tragedy of his past. Another friend, Eden Montgomery, who I first worked with in the Ukraine, literally ran away from home, but instead of joining the circus she joined PMA and was able to work through her personal pain by helping others. And let's face it, the need to be able to help others, to make a difference in their lives, is what no doubt leads most of us into the medical profession in the first place.'

'But…?' she prompted, knowing he wasn't going to let this subject drop until he'd made his point.

'But out here, working with a very close-knit group of people, providing care for literally hundreds and hundreds of people on a weekly basis, means that we need to be open with each other, that we need to rely on each other, to trust each other. Relationships in big teaching hospitals can take years to evolve, but out here they take a matter of days, sometimes…' he spread his hands wide as though to indicate the two of them '…a matter of hours, especially if there are mudslides involved.' His lips twitched into a smile at the last words. 'My point is that we're all in this together and you need to know that not only are we here as a team to provide medical care to those who need it, we're also here to help one another.'

'So you're saying that working here has helped you get over your wife's death?' She sounded sceptical but he didn't pursue it.

'Not "get over" her death but to at least come to terms with it, to accept the finality of it, yes, and I couldn't have done that without the support of those around me.' He paused, hoping he was getting through to her. 'I miss B'lana. That will never change. But I've managed to move on with my life, and I did it in stages. I'm not ready to move on in a romantic sense but time and understanding friends do go a long way to help heal the gaping holes in my life, especially when I feel raw from being split in two.' He indicated the tree beside them. 'Coming to Tarparnii has been the next stage in your life and you've done it so you can start to deal with the pains of your past.

'I'm not asking for a complete rundown of your entire history, Melora, but it's clear you're hurting, it's clear that your life has been fractured in some way. The areas of your life that can have a direct impact on your job here are what I'm asking you to be open about. If I know, I can help. If you have difficulties being around babies, I'll make sure your case load contains a lot of old men.'

He smiled and she nodded, knowing he had a point but not at all sure she could actually just blurt out the truth and tell him what was really wrong.

Melora's previous anger towards him started to fade. 'You're right that people in big teaching hospitals can take years to form any sort of lasting relationships.' Her throat went dry and she swallowed a few times and licked her lips. 'I feel as though I know you better than half the people I've been working with for years,' she said, thinking directly of Leighton. She'd been engaged to the man for two years and in the end she'd realised she'd never really known him at all. 'It's a very strange sensation.'

'Out here, we're all each other has,' he agreed, and knowing that he'd nudged her enough for the moment took a mental step back to wait. He'd watched the defensive anger she'd pulled around her start to vanish but in its place came a hesitant wariness.

A few minutes ticked by and when she didn't speak he wondered if he'd backed off too far. He was just about to talk again when she bent and picked a wild flower and started plucking the petals from it.

'My life has been split in two, just like that tree, and sometimes it feels as though it's in even more pieces than that. It's as though someone has plucked all of my petals, just like this flower. Different parts of me, the *old* parts of me, have been crushed up and scattered in the wind and I don't know if I'll ever get them all back, no matter how hard I strive for normality.'

Daniel waited, surprised at the elation he felt that she'd decided to trust him, that she'd started to open up. He knew she wouldn't tell him every-thing, but it was a first step, the tip of the iceberg, and at the moment that was all he needed so they could both do their jobs properly.

'I just want you to know, though, that I've passed all my medicals, that PMA and my surgeons have cleared me to come and work here.'

Her surgeons? That startled him a little. 'You were sick?'

'Yes.' She was still looking at the destroyed flower in her hand, feeling as though it really did signify her life. 'This morning I was in Australia, getting ready to embark on a new and very different adventure, which has brought me here— standing on a valley floor, next to a tree with so much essence and character, trying to find the right words to describe what's happened to me without boring you with all the nitty-gritty details. It's been the strangest, most exhilarating and emotionally draining day I've ever had.'

'I can believe it and, just for the record, it's not every day that we get large mudslides. I know you're probably tired and want to lie down for a while and rest, but this is important, Melora. You're only here for two weeks and I'd like those weeks to be full of healing, for both you and the patients, but also for it to be enjoyable as well.'

Melora nodded, knowing all she needed to do

was to tell Daniel enough of her turmoil so that he could structure the PMA workload while still maintaining an overall level of privacy and control. If she told him too much, too soon about her obliterated life, he'd end up feeling sorry for her and would probably remove her from the duty rosters all together.

He was looking at her now, watching her closely as she plucked another flower, blowing the petals into the wind. Was that really what her life felt like? As though she'd been plucked, her life broken up into pieces and scattered on the breeze?

Being a diagnostician, he mentally worked through a few different scenarios in his mind, watching as she tried to find the right words to tell him what had been upsetting her. She'd been sick. Perhaps she'd lost someone close to her, a child maybe. No. He dismissed that because he'd seen the way she'd eagerly held baby J'torek, kissing the child's forehead with heart-felt love. Besides, she was the one who had been sick. She'd had surgeons.

He looked at her hair. It was still short. Not extremely short but from the light, feathery way in which it was styled, he did wonder whether

her present hairstyle had something to do with chemotherapy.

'I didn't mean to cry,' she ventured. 'Earlier, when J'tana was first feeding the baby,' she quickly clarified. 'The emotions caught me completely unawares.'

'Understood.'

'I thought I'd dealt with a lot of this.'

'Sometimes emotions do tend to catch us on the hop.' She was stalling. He could see it and as she tugged at the hem of her shirt, her other hand flying to ensure the collar was down and the scarf was secure, he thought about letting her off the hook. After fidgeting, she crossed her arms protectively over her chest and he wondered why such a beautiful woman with such a slim build hid herself behind such baggy shirts.

'I can do my job, you know.' She was starting to clam up, to batten down the hatches, and Daniel's thought processes sped up. He'd taken her to the edge of the cliff and she'd thought about jumping off, of opening up to him, but now she was backing away, deciding she didn't want to do this at all. He hated to push, but he felt compelled to do it in this instance—one of his famous gut reactions he'd learned to trust over the years.

'Have you had cancer?' he asked almost before she'd finished speaking.

The colour instantly drained from her face and she felt as though the world had started to spin in the opposite direction.

'You can tell!'

CHAPTER FOUR

'OH, MY goodness!' Melora found it difficult to breathe. 'You can *tell*?' Her hands started to tremble and she clasped them together. It didn't do any good.

How could he tell? Had her prosthetic breast slipped out of line beneath her shirt? Had she accidentally knocked it? Panic and mortification continued to rise within her. She was still so new to this, was still coming to terms with everything that had happened to her during the past twenty months, but she'd also thought she was getting better at dealing with the emotional angle. Obviously not.

She shook her head and bit her lip. Daniel was talking to her, saying words, but she couldn't hear him, couldn't make out what he was saying because the drumming of her heart was reverberating around her body. Even though she was standing out in the middle of nowhere, she felt as though the world was closing in on her.

Looking up at the sky, it started to swirl around,

making her feel sick. She looked down at the ground but it was doing the same thing. How had this happened? How could he tell? Could he see? Was it that obvious? Bile rose in her throat. She squinted and tried to focus but nothing seemed to be standing still. Not the sky, not the ground, not the split-in-two tree. She felt herself pitching forward and blindly put out a hand to try and stop herself from falling over.

'Whoa, there,' she heard Daniel say, and then felt his warm arms come around her body, holding her close. 'Steady there, Melora.' His words were close to her ear, deep and rich and soothingly nice. She closed her eyes, starting to feel a bit better as she leaned into him. He adjusted his hold on her, shifting so she rested her head against his chest.

She knew she should tell him to let her go but she didn't. Standing there, waiting for the world to stop spinning, she felt secure and protected in Daniel's arms. It was an odd sensation, to feel protected by someone she really didn't know. She'd spent years with Leighton, their relationship gradually moving from colleagues to friends to a much deeper friendship before he'd proposed, and yet she'd never once felt protected by him.

Of course, that had been BC—before cancer—

when her world had been under her complete control. Now, though, it felt as though it was completely out of control. Daniel could tell she'd had breast cancer! She had no idea how he knew but as the world stopped spinning and her mind cleared from her instant panic, she knew she had to face him.

With her thoughts gradually returning to normal, Melora breathed slowly and deeply, her senses tantalised by Daniel's earthy, spicy scent. It teased around her, mixing easily with the sweet fresh fragrance she wore, blending into an exotic combination.

He smelled so nice and even though her breathing was almost back to normal and she was sure her legs would support her once again, Melora lingered for a few seconds longer, allowing his protective warmth to flood through her body.

Leaning into him, feeling calm and protected for the first time since her world had been turned upside down. For this brief snatched moment, Melora felt as though it was possible to get her head above water. It was long enough for her to take a much-needed breath and it was all because her new colleague had made her feel safe.

'You smell really nice,' she murmured, knowing

it was time to pull back, to let this brief moment go.

'So do you,' he replied, his tone deep, rumbly and sexy. It wasn't until his words penetrated her mind that she realised she'd actually spoken out loud. She instantly pushed herself away from him, his arms falling back to his sides as she stepped back, horror swamping her that she'd actually spoken those words out loud!

She stood there, staring at Daniel, her hands coming to her cheeks to feel the heat gathering there. Why had she spoken out loud? She swallowed, unsure what to do or say next.

'It's amazing that after travelling, assisting with an emergency and the lack of running water in the village, you still smell as fresh as a daisy,' he said into the temporary silence, picking up on the fact that Melora was feeling rather out of her depth at the moment.

For some reason, the fact that he'd guessed she'd had cancer had put her into a tailspin. It had just been a guess and, sadly, not a difficult one in this day and age. Even then, he was still unsure exactly what type of cancer she'd had.

Physically recovering from cancer was one thing but dealing with the emotional side-effects was something completely different and could take years to overcome. Any long-term, terminal illness could have the same effect. That was something he knew all too well, having nursed B'lana through her own terminal illness. For Melora to come to a new country, intent on new experiences, showed gumption.

Without a word, she started walking, heading away from the tree, back to the trail. Unable to look at Daniel, knowing his words had been an effort to try and bring their worlds back onto a more even keel, Melora simply wanted to get back to the village where there were other people about.

'Melora?'

He reached out a hand to her but she managed to evade his touch, her body still heated from before. Furious with herself for letting him see her like this, angry that he'd brought her out here in the first place, embarrassed that she'd almost fainted and that he'd saved her, she simply wanted to return to the village.

She reached the well-worn path and started to pick up the pace.

'Melora?' he called again, coming after her and putting his hand on her elbow to stop her. She spun around to pin him with a glare.

'What is it, Daniel?' she demanded, trying to call on the cool, calm and professional demeanour she usually wore.

'You're going the wrong way.' He pointed in the direction she was headed. 'This path takes you to the waterhole.' He jerked his other thumb in the opposite direction. '*That's* the way back to the village.'

'Oh.' Closing her eyes and clenching her teeth together, unable to believe she was behaving so irrationally, Melora took a steadying breath before looking at him. 'I'm sorry, Daniel. I don't usually act this way.' She shook her head. 'I'm usually quite poised and in control but...'

'Cancer has a way of changing all of that,' he offered.

'Yes. I've come here to Tarparnii because even though it's almost two years since I had the initial surgery and even though I've returned to work at the hospital, I have since discovered that my life, the life I had before the cancer, just doesn't seem to fit me any more.'

She paused for a moment. 'It's not really a big secret, I guess. I'm just a private person and for a while I was number one on the hospital gossip hit parade with everyone knowing I'd had breast cancer. I guess you just…took me by surprise when you guessed.'

Daniel kept his expression neutral. Breast cancer? She'd had breast cancer! His mind played back over her earlier mortification when he'd 'guessed' why she'd been sick. Had she thought he could *see* that she'd had a mastectomy? That hadn't been the case at all. Now, though, wasn't the time to tell her that. She was on a roll. She was talking and he wasn't about to stop her.

She looked down at the baggy shirt she was wearing. 'I don't know *how* you could tell. Maybe you're a superhero doctor with X-ray vision.' Her attempt at humour fell flat and she cleared her throat.

'Coming here, to this beautiful country, I thought I'd be able to get away from everything. To get away from being talked about, from everyone knowing my business, like how I coped with the last lot of chemotherapy, or that my platelet count was low this week, or that today Dr Washington's having a blood transfusion.

'It's very difficult,' she continued, 'to try and get on with your life when you have a constant barrage of "How *are* you, Melora?" being asked everywhere you go.'

'People care about you. That's good.'

'I guess.' Melora sighed heavily.

'But when everyone continually asks you "How are you?" it can become very draining,' he continued, and she turned to look at him more closely. His dark eyes were filled with sadness.

'Exactly.'

Daniel nodded. 'The same thing happens when someone you love dies.'

'Of course. So you know how it feels to not really *know* where you fit within your own world?'

'I do.'

'My world felt as though it was starting to implode. It came to the point of me not wanting to go to work, not wanting to see patients, not wanting to practise medicine any more. I felt as though I was turning into an ice queen, distancing myself from everyone, unsure who to trust, unable to find any sort of satisfaction with my life.'

'PCS. Post-cancer stress.'

'Yes. I realise that now but before Emmy suggested I come to Tarparnii, I wasn't sure what to do. So I guess I need to confess that I'm not only here to work with PMA but also to find out who I am.'

Daniel smiled. 'A noble quest.'

Melora felt the tension and earlier anxiety seep from her and sighed. Daniel knew what had happened to her and it appeared not to concern him. She was here to work, to do a job, and that was what she would do.

'Feel better?'

'Surprisingly, yes.'

'Shall we?' he asked, indicating the correct way back to the village.

'Yes. Thank you.'

As they walked, Daniel pointed out other different things. Chatting to Melora, sharing more of his land with her, meant he didn't have to think about the intense couple of moments they'd shared—of seeing the mortification cross her face, of seeing the panic in her eyes just before she'd almost fainted and ended up in his arms. Holding her close, supporting her, feeling the pain emanating from her, Daniel had wanted to help her, to hold her, to protect her. She was a woman who'd been through a lot and yet she was still soldiering on.

He admired her for that.

'Everything out here is so incredibly different.' There was utter delight in her tone. 'The colours, the smells, the—'

Daniel put his arm out in front of her to stop her walking. 'Wait.'

'Daniel?'

'Shh. Don't move.' His words were quiet but direct and Melora's alarm bells instantly started to ring. She quickly looked around them, trying to figure out what was going on…and then she saw it. A large, thick, snake crossing the path not too far from where they were. A cold sweat settled over her and her mouth went instantly dry.

'What do we do?' She clutched at his arm, needing the security of being close to him.

'Just stay right where you are. Don't move.'

Melora kept her eyes fixed to the snake, unsure in which direction it was travelling as she could see neither the head nor the tail. 'Is it…deadly?' In her research she had come across information about snakes and the different types that were indigenous to Tarparnii but right now, for the life of her, she was unable to recall any of the information as fear had become her dominant emotion.

'Very.'

'Do we just wait for it to go?'

'No.' There was determination mixed with a hint of regret in Daniel's tone. 'It's too close to the village.' He dropped his arm and she immediately clutched her hands together, holding them close to her chest as her heart pounded wildly.

Shivers ran down Melora's spine and as Daniel moved away from her towards the snake she instinctively reached out a hand to stop him. 'Daniel,' she whispered, her concern more than evident in her tone.

He glanced back at her and smiled. 'Relax. I've done this hundreds of times.'

'Done what?' Her eyes widened as she watched him head off the path and into the scrub, pulling the hunting knife, which she'd completely forgotten he wore, from the pouch at his waist. 'Oh, my goodness.' She swallowed over the terror in her throat and stood exactly where she was, following his instructions to the letter.

Her eyes were almost bugging out of her head, and her hands now up at her mouth as Daniel disappeared completely from her view. She could hear him, his gentle and careful footfalls before the sound of a loud *thwack* reverberated around them.

She screamed at the sound, shoving her hands almost into her mouth in an effort to keep herself quiet. The length of snake still visible on the path started to wiggle and squirm and although Melora wanted nothing more than to close her eyes, to be anywhere except where she was, standing still on a slightly overgrown path in the middle of a jungle, she kept her gaze firmly fixed on the reptile. There was another thud and then the snake's body moved extremely fast towards the direction Daniel had taken.

Her heart rate was all but off the chart with fear and trepidation as she stood there, waiting. A minute later, she couldn't take the suspense and uncertainty any more. 'Daniel?' she called.

'It's fine. I'm fine,' he returned, and instantly appeared at the edge of the path. 'Sorry. Didn't mean to frighten you.' He had his hunting knife in his hand, the blade tinged with what she presumed to be bits of snake.

'Ugh.' Shuddering again, she looked at him. 'Can I move now?'

'Yes. It's all safe. No more snake. Well…' he said as he stepped over a fallen tree branch onto the path, the snake's body in his free hand, 'no more *alive* snake. It won't be bothering the village this evening, except as an accompaniment to tonight's meal.'

Melora shook her head in utter astonishment and swallowed over the bubble of hysteria she could feel rising up. 'Oh, well…that's OK, then,' she re-marked with a nervous laugh.

'Shall we head back?' He inclined his head to-wards the village.

'You're not dull to be around. I'll give you that,' she said, walking quickly past him. He stayed a few steps behind her, dragging the snake's dead body after them. Melora glanced at it more than once.

'What type of snake was it?'

'Green-belly ringed snake. Sort of the Tarparniian equivalent to the boa constrictor. They don't usu-ally come this close to the village but when they do, we need to get rid of them quickly. Also, they're the ones that taste best.'

Melora laughed in disbelief. 'You're wild, Daniel Tarvon.'

'Actually, I'm just your typical Tarparniian-Englishman who has vowed to protect new PMA staff from snakes, mudslides and anything else that might come along.' He chuckled, the sound washing over her, relaxing her previous tension and giving her that same light-heartedness she'd expe-rienced after the mudslide adventure had ended.

As they entered the village, Daniel's green-belly ringed snake instantly became the centre of attention, Melora wondered who was going to protect her against the awe and sensual attraction she most definitely felt for her new colleague.

That night, as it turned out, was a special night in the village.

'It's a welcoming banquet,' Daniel told her after he'd washed up from handling the snake. They were sitting in the food hut, chopping up fruit. Simone and two other children had insisted on helping and were putting the chopped fruit onto wooden platters. The little girl declared that she would sit next to Melora while they worked.

''Cos we're yellow girls.' She giggled, referring to the colour of their hair, and that was that.

'What's a welcoming banquet?' Melora asked. 'Is someone important coming to the village?'

'Yes.' Daniel glanced across the table then pointed to her. 'You.'

Melora stopped chopping and met his gaze. '*Me*? Oh, no. I don't need a big welcoming banquet. They don't need to do that. There doesn't need to be any fuss for me.'

'It's their custom, Melora. The village welcome all new PMA doctors, on behalf of the Tarparniian people, as a small token of their thanks. It would be extremely ungracious of you to refuse and they would take great umbrage.'

'And they do this for everyone who comes?'

'Yes. They don't have much but what they do have, they're more than willing to share.'

She looked around the food hut, seeing women preparing food, kneading a bread-type dough and generally getting things ready. She shook her head slowly, amazed at the generosity of these people. 'They make me feel very humble. I'm sure I don't deserve it.'

'I'm sure you do.' Daniel smiled. 'Usually, we have a group of people arriving from PMA to help out and they all get welcomed in just the same way. As it turns out, this time it's just you coming into this little world and, as such, you deserve the official welcome. Of course, that doesn't mean you get out of helping.' He pointed to the fruit in front of her. 'Now chop, Dr Washington!'

As the sun started to set, Melora found it difficult to believe so much had happened to her since she'd risen early that morning back at her apartment in Australia. In some ways, it felt as though she'd been here in Tarparnii for much longer than just today. While exhaustion was starting to set in, she was eager for the celebrations to begin.

The bonfire was lit, food was passed around, children clapped and laughed, singing songs with the help of one of the PMA crew, Sue, who played the guitar. Meeree and Jalak officially welcomed her to their village and where she thought she'd feel highly self-conscious, standing out from the crowd with her blonde hair and inexperience of their way of life, she didn't feel at all like an interloper but rather as though she'd just been accepted into a loving family.

It warmed her heart and humbled her at the same time.

Throughout the evening Daniel was attentive by her side, introducing her to the other PMA staff members, some of whom had come from the United Kingdom and New Zealand and some who, like Daniel, lived in the village, such as Belhara, their resident anaesthetist, and Bel, a Tarparniian nurse.

Daniel was her anchor in this foreign world and she would turn to him with questions and comments and he would always provide whatever answer she needed.

'How are you feeling?' he asked as Melora sipped at her drink. 'Tired?'

'Yes, but it's a good tired.' She nodded. Simone

ran past them at that point, laughing and playing games with her friends. The young girl had been particularly attentive towards Melora that evening, often telling anyone who would listen that there was someone else in the village just like her—someone with yellow hair. The child seemed happy, relieved in some ways, to no longer be the odd one out, and the hair colour connection had instantly bonded them.

'Simone is simply gorgeous, Daniel. She's a credit to you.'

'Thank you, Mel. That means a lot.'

'Mel?' It wasn't the first time he'd called her that today.

'Do you not like it?'

'I don't mind it. It's what my closest friends sometimes call me.'

He shifted on the wooden bench they sat on, coming physically closer to her. 'Is this close enough?' he joked, his voice laced with ironic humour.

'It's too close.' She gave a nervous chuckle and edged away, wishing he wouldn't do things like that because it only served to remind her of how incredible he really was. Although, when she thought about it, could he really be as wonderful as he appeared? Everyone had flaws but she was yet to discover what Daniel's were.

'Fair enough,' he murmured, and eased back. 'But I can still call you Mel, right? I mean, we've shared quite a bit today.'

'We have.' She nodded as Simone came running up to them.

'Melora?' she began in that sing-song tone of hers, clambering up onto Melora's knee.

'Yes?' She put her arms around the little girl and held her close, loving the feel of the small body against her own. She was still astonished that this child, a stranger, had taken such a shine to her. It was incredibly nice as well as flattering, and with the way her ego had been dented in the past, she would take all the flattery she could get.

'Will you…' Simone yawned '…read me a story?'

'Oh.' She was a little surprised at the request. 'Uh…of course.'

'Good.' Simone leaned into her, shifting to put her legs out along the bench, her feet resting on her father's knee. 'I'll get the book soon.'

'OK.' Melora rested her chin on Simone's head and looked over at Daniel. 'What were we talking about?' As she asked the question, she felt a yawn begin to rise and quickly smothered it.

'Simone's started you off,' Daniel joked. 'You must be exhausted, Melora.'

'I don't know, between mudslides, births and snakes, you would have thought I'd have an extra barrel of energy somewhere.'

'I think you've already used it up.' He looked at the two of them, the 'bright' girls with their shiny blonde hair. 'You've really made her day. Thank you.'

'For having the same colour hair? I assure you, I didn't plan it.'

His soft chuckle washed over her. 'Thanks all the same. As a doting father, I like seeing my daughter happy. It doesn't take much to put a smile on her face but when it's there, it's as though all is right with my world.' There was a wistfulness in his tone.

'How long ago did your wife die?' she couldn't help but ask.

'Just after Simone turned one.'

'Meeree mentioned you were in England?'

'That's right. B'lana had been diagnosed with a Tarparniian disease known as *Olhano Sigdesh*.'

'I've never heard of it.'

'I wouldn't expect you would. Even here in Tarparnii it's not all that common. It's a disease that attacks the immune system, much like leukaemia or Mediterranean fever. By the time I was able to pinpoint what was wrong she was already pregnant with Simone. Treatment would have cured her but killed the baby. B'lana refused to let anything happen to our child. It was a difficult decision for her to make…but now, almost four years later, only now am I starting to feel as though I have my life back on firmer ground.'

And that, more than anything, was the perfect reason why Melora knew she had to keep her distance from this man who was interesting, intriguing and incredibly sexy. He was handsome, rugged and had a fantastic sense of humour. After everything that had happened today, she trusted him, and her trust was not something she gave away willy-nilly.

'Simone helped to get you through the toughest times?' Melora asked before smothering another yawn. The child in her arms hadn't moved, hadn't run off to get the story book and instead was deadweight, obviously sound asleep.

'She did. If I hadn't had Simone to concentrate on during those first few months after B'lana's death,

I most certainly wouldn't have coped. Here, let me take her. She can get quite heavy.' He shifted Simone's feet off his knee and stood to take his sleeping child from Melora.

'Time to turn in,' Daniel announced. 'You have a busy day ahead of you tomorrow, Dr Washington, and you're going to need all the rest you can get.'

Melora put her hand across her mouth as she yawned again, relieved he'd taken Simone from her but sad that her cuddle had come to an end. She twirled her wrists and stretched her arms as she stood. 'Earlier on, I did wonder whether I'd be able to sleep tonight but the fact that I'm now completely exhausted will no doubt assist in that area.'

Daniel shifted his daughter so her head lay on his shoulder, her arms about his neck. 'You'll sleep. Most definitely.'

'Great. Has anyone figured out exactly where I'm supposed to sleep?' she asked as they walked quietly towards the huts. 'I'm presuming my bag is wherever I'm headed.'

'Yes.'

'Great. I'm looking forward to changing out of

these clothes. So which hut is yours?' she asked as they strolled along.

'The one down the end. Simone and I share with the supply hut.'

Her smile was instant. 'Oh, how delightful for you both.'

'It's not that bad. Supplies are at the front, Simone and I are at the back. We'll shift some boxes and crates around and make some room for you.'

'I'm to sleep in *your* hut?' She was gobsmacked. 'I uh...I hadn't realised.' And why was she getting all jittery about it? It was a hut. Somewhere to sleep. She needed to be practical about it but all she kept thinking was that she didn't want to share a place with Daniel for the next two weeks. The man was affecting her far more than she liked and now she was going to have to deal with sleeping in the same hut as him, with only a four year old girl as chaperone? Not that they needed a chaperone, she added quickly, mainly because nothing was going to happen between them.

Attractions could be fought. Exhaustion couldn't—at least, not now. Melora yawned again. She would start fighting tomorrow.

CHAPTER FIVE

THERE was pain. She had pain and it didn't seem to be going away.

Although Melora had been exhausted after her exceedingly full day, she was roused from her sleep due to pain in her left arm. When she tried to sit up, to figure out why her arm had no blood flow, she was astonished to find Simone had snuggled close to her and was resting her heavy little head on Melora's arm. She lay back down and sighed, wondering how to extract the child without waking her up.

'Something wrong?' Daniel's tone on the other side of Simone had been bleary, indicating he was half-asleep himself.

'No. Sorry. Didn't mean to wake you.'

'I was dozing. Are you not comfortable? The sleeping mats and bedding do take a while to get used to, especially if you're used to a soft mattress with lots of cuddly blankets on top.'

'No. It's all fine.'

'You're warm enough? Or cool enough?'

'I'm in a perfect state of warmness.' She smiled at his words. 'It's not that.'

Daniel eased up onto his elbow, the sheet which had been across him sliding down to reveal a dark, naked chest. There wasn't much light in the room, only that afforded by the half-moon outside, but even amongst the shadows Melora could tell that he was a man who definitely kept in good shape. 'What's the problem?'

No sooner had he propped himself up on his elbow and looked across at her than he realised what had happened. Without worrying about waking his daughter, he reached out and shifted the little body back towards him, resting Simone's head on the frilly pink pillow that was, no doubt, Simone's pride and joy.

'Sorry about that. She's a real cuddler. I often wake up with dead arms and quite a few times she either has her head on my chest or right up against my face.' He chuckled into the darkness, still looking over at Melora. 'It's a bit disconcerting when the first thing you see when you open your eyes in the morning are two big brown eyes staring directly into yours only a hair's-breadth away.'

Melora was rubbing her arm, trying to get blood

flow back into it. 'I wasn't sure if I could move her or not. I thought she might wake up.'

'Ha! Once Simone's out she's out for the count, but be warned, she wakes very early. It's almost as though she can sense the first rays of the sun hitting the earth. Half the time I think it's Simone who wakes the birds up, rather than the other way around.' He pushed his long, loose hair back from his face, highlighting the angles and rugged jaw, and she found it difficult not to stare.

Melora smiled at his words and turned to lie on her side, the pins and needles in her arm now starting to settle down but the butterflies in her stomach starting to take flight. What was it about this man that seemed to send her hormones off into a right old tizz? 'It's nice to see a father who's so close to his daughter.'

'Thanks.' He reached out a hand and brushed hair back from Simone's face. 'She's my world.'

His words were so rich, so deep, so powerful that Melora's throat instantly choked over. Daniel slowly shook his head. 'She's my world and yet I need to destroy hers.'

'What?' She frowned. 'Why?'

Daniel exhaled slowly. 'She's getting older. She'll need more soon. More than just running around the village enjoying the carefree existence she thinks is her life.'

'School?'

'Yes.'

'Don't they have schools here?'

'They do…' Daniel lay back and laced his hands behind his head, looking up at the thatched roof '…but academic excellence isn't all that important to Tarparniians.'

Melora shifted up onto her elbow so she could see him a little better, then immediately wished she hadn't as the outline of his arm muscles was intense. 'It's normal…' she started, and had to clear her throat as her words had come out all sleepy and husky.

'It's normal,' she tried again, 'for a father to want the best for his child. Of course you want Simone to have a good education. Think of all the different ways she'd be able to help out here in Tarparnii when she's older if she's been properly educated.'

'But is it really *that* important? Why can't she be like the other children here? Like Belhara's children? Going to the local school, learning the basics and also being a functioning member of this village—*her* village?'

'Because you have the means, the knowledge and the understanding to know there is more for her. Belhara told me he was trained by PMA staff to be an anaesthetist, that he'd studied tribal medicine but that through PMA training him, he can help out more for his people.'

'He told you that?' Daniel was a little surprised.

'Yes. At the welcome banquet.'

'Where was I?'

'I think you were off getting me another drink, which you didn't need to do, by the way. I was more than capable of looking after myself.'

'I was being a polite host,' he countered.

Melora smiled. 'And I thank you for it, kind sir.'

'I should think so,' he muttered, but she could hear the humour in his words. They fell silent again and Melora lay down again, looking across at Simone and Daniel.

'I don't know if I can send her away to school. My father did that to me. Ripped me away from my mother, from my life here, and dumped me in a boarding school.' There was pain and anguish in his tone and he shook his head. 'That first year, so young, so alone, so terrified...' He trailed off, not bothering to finish his sentence because the desolation in his voice was evident and enough to convey into the silence how much pain he'd experienced. 'I can't do that to her.'

'Then you'll find an alternative, Daniel. Simone *is* your world. That's clear even to me and I've only known you both a day. You're right to be really thinking things through and you'll find a solution.' Simone shifted again and this time turned towards her father, cuddling in close, his arms coming about his child in a firm and protective manner. 'You'll do what's right for both of you.'

They were silent for a while and Melora had just closed her eyes when he spoke again.

'Thanks, Melora. I needed to hear that.'

She kept her eyes closed but smiled, sighing contentedly as sleep once more started to claim her. 'Any time.'

With that, Daniel heard her breathing even out, indicating she'd gone back to sleep. He lay there, in the stillness of pre-dawn, unable to believe how much better he felt after talking to Melora. She had confidence in him, confidence that he would make the right decision, that he would do what was best for himself and Simone.

It was a nice feeling to have, given that since

B'lana's death he'd simply seemed to muddle through from one day to the next, learning as he went. Toilet training, manners, feeding times, teething, inquisitiveness. Although he'd had help from those around him in the village, although he knew that Simone belonged to everyone, as did all of the other children in the village, the adults always caring and teaching and protecting their own, *he* was her father and at the end of the day *he* was the one to make the hard decisions.

'You'll do what's right for both of you.' Melora's words hung in the air and slowly Daniel closed his eyes. This woman, this new woman who had herself been through a very traumatic time, believed in him and it made him feel great.

True to his word, Daniel had his team up and ready to work well before seven o'clock the next morning. Melora was surprised to see patients emerging from the forests surrounding the village at such an early hour, lining up in an orderly fashion outside the clinic building.

'P'Ko-lat is our receptionist-cum-triage nurse so she's the one making sense of the variety of patients we'll see,' Daniel said as they exited the food hut with Keith, an orthopaedic Maori doctor from New Zealand hard on their heels. Richard, an obstetrician from the UK, had already gone into the clinic with Sue, an Australian nurse from Perth.

She was keeping her distance from Daniel this morning, his powerful presence only adding to her awareness of him. Melora had been talking to Bel when Daniel had first entered the food hut that morning, surrounded by Simone and her friends. He'd organised the children, sitting them down at the long wooden tables and making sure they all had something to eat before finally sitting down with his own breakfast.

He'd glanced her way once and smiled, his brown eyes deep and expressive, but then Simone had accidentally spilt her drink and he'd quickly set about cleaning it up. As she'd watched him talk to his daughter and the rest of the children, she'd been able to see what a wonderful, caring father he was. Although he had help from the rest of the village, there was something about the way he held Simone, the way he pressed a kiss to her head, lingering slightly and closing his eyes as though he wanted to capture that single moment in time. He loved his daughter It was plain for everyone to see and Melora had been touched with his dedication as a father.

'If you need any help with translating,' Daniel continued, bringing her thoughts back to the present, 'ask P'Ko-lat—or Meeree is usually around, helping out. Everything you need should be in the examination area but I'll quickly go over things now with you so hopefully you won't feel as though we're throwing you in at the deep end…especially as you didn't pack a bathing suit,' he couldn't help but tease, and his words went a long way to helping ease her nervous tension.

'Very funny, Tarvon. Are you always this witty with your newest recruits? Trying to make them feel less flustered by teasing them a little?'

'It's working, isn't it?' They entered one of the small examination rooms, Daniel grinning his gorgeous, heart-stopping grin at her. 'Bathing suit or not, I think you're going to do brilliantly, Melora. Right.' He put one hand on the cupboard and opened the door. 'Supplies. What you have in here should last you the entire clinic. You'll have plenty of people needing immunisations, others requiring debridement and bandaging of wounds, mostly general first aid.

'I tend to get most of the eye cases as I've become

an expert over the years, Richard will take most of the pregnant women, Keith will have any patients with broken bones but we all see a general mix. P'Ko-lat is good at recognising our individual strengths and tailoring the patient's needs with the necessary health-care provider. If you *do* get a case you're unsure of, interrupt whoever you need. We're all here to help each other help the people. We're a team.'

'No "I" in team. Got it, boss.'

Daniel smiled and shook his head. 'Sorry. Didn't mean to get carried away with the pep talk. Just want you to know your parameters.' He quickly pointed out a few more things in the room before walking to the door. 'All right, Mel.' He nodded then gave her a mock salute. 'See you on the other side of clinic!'

'Once more into the fray?'

Daniel's spontaneous laughter vibrated through her and she couldn't help but smile in return, desperately ignoring the way her world seemed a little brighter when he was around. 'Precisely.' With that, he headed off to his own examination room. No sooner had he left than P'Ko-lat came through with a patient, explaining to Melora the problem.

That set up the rhythm for the rest of the clinic,

with Meeree and P'Ko-lat working together to make sure she knew what each patient required. Melora wrote notes for every patient, as was the clinic's practice, and just when she thought there couldn't possibly be any more patients who required attention, another wave seemed to appear from nowhere and in they'd come.

At some point someone brought her a warm drink and some fruit, for which she was very grateful, and later that night she literally fell into bed, doubly exhausted from two very hectic days. Where she'd felt a little self-conscious sleeping in the hut with Daniel and his daughter the night before, tonight she didn't feel nearly as concerned. It was a great sensation and when Simone asked for a cuddle, Melora instantly opened her arms, delighted to have been accepted so easily by this child.

'She really likes you,' Daniel murmured, both of them yawning with exhaustion.

'The feeling's mutual.'

'She's never really bonded with any of the other women in this way. Of course she likes them and cuddles them but with you it seems to be different.'

Melora breathed in Simone's scent and relaxed. 'It's the hair colour.' She yawned, her words a little slurred, indicating she was on the verge of sleep. 'It has the power to make me stand out from the crowd, to have babies named after it and attract other blonde little girls.' She chuckled at her own silliness and Daniel smiled.

'Mel?' he said a few minutes later, but received no reply. 'Melora?' He looked over at the two blonde-haired beauties and wondered whether he should be concerned. Simone had attached herself to Melora within minutes of meeting her but there was something else... Was Simone trying to tell him that she needed a mother? That although she was well cared for within the village that she still wanted a mother of her own?

Melora would be gone in just two weeks' time, out of their lives for goodness knew how long. Would she ever come back to help again in Tarparnii? Would she settle down to her life in Sydney, having found the level of inner peace she was searching for? Was it right for him to allow Simone to become close to this woman who would leave?

Daniel knew he couldn't protect Simone from every pain the world would throw at her but as a father it was his job to be concerned.

* * *

Melora was up bright and early, and she and Simone were able to tiptoe out of the hut without waking Daniel, the two of them giggling together as they ran to the food hut. That's where Daniel found the two of them about twenty minutes later. Melora was sitting next to Simone, reading a book out loud while nibbling on some fruit and honey mixed with goat's milk yoghurt. He stopped before they saw him, watching the two fair-haired beauties engrossed in the story he must have read to Simone over a hundred times.

She loved that book. It had been one of the ones B'lana had bought as they'd prepared the nursery together at his apartment in Bath. The story was about a little girl who wasn't afraid to go to school, to take a step outside her comfort zone, because she had support from her family and friends.

'You'll read it to her when she's older,' B'lana had said to him as she'd caressed her belly.

'Don't talk like that,' he'd answered. 'You'll make it through. We'll find a cure.'

B'lana had merely shaken her head and smiled at him in that indulgent way that said she knew he was wrong but she was more than willing to humour him.

'Find someone.' Those had been some of the last

words his wife had said to him, almost four years ago. 'There is someone else out there for you to love, Daniel. Someone who will be good for you and for our Simone.'

'*No!*' The word had been wrenched from him and tears had filled his eyes as he'd held her close, willing the life that he could feel slipping from her body to instantly return.

Simone giggled and clapped her hands, bringing Daniel's thoughts back to the present. He blinked away the past and watched as his daughter looked up at Melora.

'Again?'

Melora's only response was to raise a stern eyebrow, indicating Simone had forgotten something.

'Please, Melora?' Simone batted her eyelashes as well, hoping that sweet and cute might work as well as manners.

'Ah, Miss Manners, there you are. Of course I'll read it again.'

Excitement bubbled through Simone and she opened the book to the first page. 'I like the way you read it. It's different from the way Daddy does it.'

'That's because we're different people with

different experiences in life, so we read the same book differently.'

Simone giggled and pointed eagerly to the first page. Melora began to read, quietly but with resounding inflection. At present they were the only two in the food hut, sitting there, absorbed in their own little blonde world, and Daniel wished he'd brought his camera with him so he could capture the two of them in a photo.

When Simone turned the page, the two of them discussed the pictures drawn to illustrate the words and Melora popped a piece of fruit into her mouth. She was reaching for her second piece when she glanced up and saw him standing there.

Their eyes met across the empty food hut, neither of them moving, both of them staring and neither of them looking away. The rotation of the earth seemed to slow down and time seemed to stand still.

He was freshly washed and clean shaven, his hair pulled back into its usual ponytail. He wore a cotton shirt, a pair of shorts and his comfortable boat shoes, the belt, complete with hunting knife, at his waist. It was his clean, fresh face that definitely caught her attention as since she'd arrived he hadn't shaved, giving him that dark and rugged and slightly dangerous look that had definitely appealed to her.

Now that she was able to see his square jaw, the clear angles of his cheekbones and the full effect of his mouth, her heart seemed to be thumping faster. If he had been wearing a three-piece suit, he'd fit right in at any high-powered hospital in the world, and yet still there was a heated sensuality to him that only enticed her further.

He really was incredibly handsome, and he appeared to be looking at her as though she were unique and wonderful and precious. It was an odd sensation, and one Melora couldn't remember ever feeling before, even when she'd been engaged to Leighton.

It brought back the memories of being held close to Daniel's firm body when she'd been in his arms, the warmth surrounding them, the world disappearing so only the two of them were left. The same sensations seemed to be surrounding them again and she was confused about what she should do next. The way he was looking at her made her heart-rate increase, made her mouth go dry and her body instantly react with a mass of tingles.

How could he evoke such a reaction with one simple look? And even then he'd accomplished it from the other side of the hut. What did it mean? It made her feel so special and very feminine, something she hadn't felt in such a long time.

Was it real or was she simply imagining things? Perhaps he wasn't looking at her at all but rather was looking at his daughter? No. Even though her mind was working three times as fast as normal to try and make sense of the multitude of girly emotions buzzing through her, Daniel was most definitely looking directly at her...as though she was really special to him.

'Mel-ora.' Simone's sing-song tone beside her burst the bubble and Melora instantly whipped her head down to look at the little girl.

'Yes? Sorry? Yes?'

'Did I scare you?' she asked with a little giggle.

'Uh...yes. Yes, you did.' Melora closed her eyes and willed her body to stop trembling with excitement and to focus on the child beside her. She didn't want to open her eyes in case she came face to face with Daniel. Maybe he'd decided against having some food and had headed off to the clinic with an empty stomach. Maybe she'd find that he hadn't been standing there at all and that she'd simply been hallucinating. One could only hope.

'Daddy!' Simone squealed, and Melora tensed for a moment. It had been real. The whole 'eyes meeting across an uncrowded room' thing had been real. Daniel had stared at her and she'd stared back at him. She hadn't imagined it at all and now she had to face the man who was starting to rattle her nerves more than she cared to admit.

'Good morning, *Separ.*' Daniel greeted his daughter. 'What are you two doing?'

When Melora opened her eyes, it was to find that Daniel was now sitting down on the opposite side of the large wooden table. The large bench seats often accommodated about eight to ten people on either side but at the moment the three of them seemed to be here in a pocket of time where there was no one else around.

'Melora is reading to me, Daddy.' Simone patted her book lovingly.

'Isn't that nice of her?' Daniel's gaze slowly travelled from his daughter, who was once more engrossed in the story, to encompass Melora. 'Thank you, Mel.'

'It…it's no big drama,' she said, cross with herself for stuttering. 'It's a great book.'

'It's my favourite,' Simone added. 'My mummy

bought it for me before she died, didn't she, Daddy?'

At the mention of Daniel's wife Melora started to feel a little uncomfortable yet she wasn't quite sure why.

'She did and she would be so happy to see that you and Melora are enjoying the story together.'

'That's nice.'

'My mummy was nice, wasn't she, Daddy?'

'She was very nice,' Daniel agreed, winking at his daughter.

'And she was pretty, just like me, wasn't she, Daddy?' Simone smoothed a hand down the blonde hair Melora had combed that morning.

'Very pretty,' he confirmed, and from his indulgent tone Melora had the feeling this wasn't the first time he'd had this conversation with his daughter. It was good that he reminisced with Simone about her mother. It was right.

Simone looked seriously at Melora. 'She died when I was one.' The little girl's lilting words indicated she'd had those same words spoken to her by someone else and was parroting them. 'She got really sick and didn't want to take the special medicine because it might hurt me, because I was in her tummy and she said she wanted her baby to be big and strong, and I *am* big and strong, just like my mummy wanted, and she did all that because she really loved me, didn't she, Daddy?' Simone nodded as though she already knew the answer.

'She *really* did,' he confirmed.

Melora was listening intently to everything Simone was saying and Tarvon wondered what she might be thinking. He looked across at her and once more their gazes seemed to meet. This time, though, there wasn't the heat or recognition of awareness he'd seen before but instead her honey eyes reflected that she was happy.

'My daddy loves me, too,' Simone told Melora, her tone still earnest.

'I can see that. You're very special to him.'

Simone tipped her head to the side. 'Am I special to you?'

Melora's heart turned over with pride at being asked such an important question. 'Of course you are. We're the girls with the yellow hair, remember?'

'Yes. We are special to each other.' Simone clapped her hands joyfully, happy to have received approval from her Melora. Daniel heard alarm bells ring somewhere in the back of his mind, warning him that it might not be all that good for Simone to form a permanent attachment to Melora, but he suppressed them.

Instead, he clapped his hands together, needing to move things along. There was another busy day ahead of them. 'Right, *Separ.*' He fixed his daughter with a look. 'If you've finished your breakfast, I suggest you go along and see Nandi. She's waiting to show you and your friends how to make bread dough today.'

'Yay.' After more clapping of the hands Simone slid down from the bench, shimmying beneath the table to pop her head up beside her father. After giving him a quick hug, she was about to break into a run when Daniel stopped her.

'Excuse me, missy. Manners, please?' He held out her book to her and inclined his head towards Melora.

'Uh? Oh, sorry.' Simone faced Melora. 'Thank you for reading to me. I did love it.'

'You're welcome. Any time.'

'How about tonight?' Simone instantly asked.

'You've done it now,' Daniel remarked in an undertone that made Melora smile.

'Sounds wonderful.'

'Yay.' Simone took the book from her father

before skipping out of the food hut, leaving the two of them alone.

'I'm not sure if you fully realise what you've just committed yourself to, Melora. My daughter is a bookworm and loves to have stories read to her. You're just lucky that for the past two nights she's been too exhausted to bother reading.'

'That's good that she likes books so much, especially for someone her age, and as I'm a bookworm, too, I think I'll cope.' She paused and then asked, 'Is this part of your plan to further her education? She speaks both Tarparniian and English fluently, she loves stories, and in loving stories she'll find reading easier to cope with.' Melora paused for a moment. 'You said there are schools out here. Why couldn't you send her to one of the village schools and then have other schoolwork sent over?'

'I've thought of that but with all the work I do with PMA, I simply don't have the time to devote to her studies, not properly, and I also don't want her to have a half-hearted education.' He shook his head. 'She has a passion for learning.'

Melora agreed. 'Children her age are usually like little sponges, all too eager to soak up knowledge.'

'True, and that's why Meeree and Jalak are also

encouraging the children here to learn English. Most times they can speak it better than their parents.'

'It's great that they want to learn. You'll sort it out,' she encouraged him again. 'She's four and three quarters, almost five, Daniel,' Melora pointed out with a cheeky smile, recalling how Simone liked her exact age to be known. 'You've got some time to figure things out.'

'The boarding school in England can take her in six months' time or else she has to wait another year.' He put his elbows on the table and covered his face with his hands, dejection in his shoulders, lifelessness in his tone.

Melora could see how badly the thought of being separated from his daughter was affecting him and desperately wanted to shimmy beneath the table herself so she could pop out the other side and comfort him. Sanity, thankfully, kicked in and she stayed where she was but couldn't resist reaching out a hand to him, touching his arm gently. 'Would it be so bad for her to go?'

'I don't want her to have the horrible time I had,' he mumbled into his hands.

'How do you know she will? You've told me that you didn't really get along with your father, and maybe that's the main difference here. You and Simone are very close, like peas in a pod, and nothing—not boarding school, not having experiences in other countries—is ever going to change that. You're not "posting" her off to boarding school to get her out of your hair, you're giving her the opportunity to have a wonderful education because you want her to have a rich and full life.'

Daniel was silent and for a moment Melora wondered whether she'd overstepped the lines of new friendships. 'Maybe that's what your father wanted to give you as well,' she continued quietly. 'He may not have known how to show his affection properly but he did give you the opportunity of a great education, and just look at what you've been able to achieve.'

He lifted his head and nodded slowly. 'You make a valid case, Dr Washington. I've always resented my father for sending me off, for making me feel as though I wasn't worthy of his time or attention, but perhaps he really didn't have any clue how to relate to me.'

'Exactly. It's completely different with you and Simone. That little girl adores her daddy. Everyone can see it and with you she really is the apple of

your eye. You relate to her, you're the most important person in her life and you love her completely,
Daniel. You're a good father.' The last words were
imploring.

'Thank you, Melora. That does mean a lot and
maybe you're right. Boarding school for Simone
would be very different because she would know I
was doing it so she could have a brilliant future.'

'And as such it also proves that you are nothing
like your father. Your motives are different, your
sincerity is real. Also, I wouldn't doubt that your
father's sincerity in ensuring you had a good education was also real.'

'He just didn't know how to express it.' As Daniel
said the words, he breathed in deeply and exhaled
slowly, as though he was letting go of heavy animosity that had been gathering deep within him
for almost four decades. 'He wanted the best for
me.'

'It's what every parent wants for their child but
some express it better than others and, besides, it's
quite clear that *you've* turned out just fine.'

He quirked an eyebrow at her, his expression
changing from one of confusion about his daughter's education to awareness of the woman before
him. The instant she saw that look in his eyes she

knew he was changing the subject, and because she felt more comfortable with him now, she let him. He captured her hand in both of his and thankfully she didn't try to pull away. 'Just fine?' he fished, the corner of his mouth twitching upwards.

'Well…better than fine.' Melora felt the proverbial ground, which had just started to settle beneath her feet, shift again. Daniel was flirting with her…and she was liking it.

'You know, you've agreed to a date with my daughter,' he said softly. 'So does that mean you'll agree to a date with me?'

'Uh…' Her throat went instantly dry at his words.

'After all, it's only right that I get to know the woman who's going to be spending time with Simone. I'm a very protective father.'

'I have no doubt about that.'

'So what do you say?'

'To what?' She was actually getting quite confused.

'To having a date with me?'

'People out here date? Where do they go? What do they do?'

'Of course they date. How else do you think marriages eventuate?'

'M-marriage?' Her eyes widened with shock. 'You want to get *married*?'

CHAPTER SIX

DANIEL's heartbeat stopped for what felt like an eternity but in reality it was just a moment.

'No! No. Did you think I was...?' He shook his head. *'No.'* He quickly stood from the bench seat and crossed his arms over his chest. He didn't want to get married again. He already had too much on his plate. Work. Simone. Feelings for Melora he didn't want to have. No. Marriage didn't figure in his future plans at all.

'You scared me.'

'You misunderstood me.' They spoke in unison, stared at each other and then both laughed, Melora placing a hand over her heart as though she was relieved.

Why was she relieved? Didn't she want to get married? Not necessarily to him but to anyone? She'd already been through so much, with her cancer and the treatments that went with it, so it was understandable, but how had she jumped the conclusion that he'd been asking her to marry him?

Was she lonely? He would have thought someone as gorgeous as Melora would have had someone waiting for her in Australia but she hadn't mentioned anyone. Maybe it had been the way he'd asked her for the date? Had he said it wrong? She was the first woman he'd asked since B'lana and maybe he'd done it wrong.

It was another example that they came from completely different worlds. His life was here in Tarparnii and *if* he ever decided to head down the path of matrimony again, it would be with someone who understood this land, who understood its customs and who loved the people.

Still, he had to admit that the prospect of getting to know Melora better, of perhaps seeing where this attraction he felt towards her might lead, was rather appealing. He looked at her, the pink tinge on her cheeks, the expressiveness of her honey-coloured eyes, the way she bit her lower lip. She was very beautiful, there was no denying that.

'Daniel?' Melora's sweet voice brought his mind back to the present and he realised he was still staring at her.

'Sorry.'

'I think we'd better head to clinic—or at least I do. The more I familiarise myself with the place, the better.' As she spoke, she carried her empty plate to the washbasin, pleased that her legs were able to support her as she cleaned up after herself. The way Daniel had looked at her when he'd first entered the food hut, the way he'd been staring at her only a moment ago, all of it—the attention, the banter, the flirting, the laughter—made her feel...pretty. And she hadn't felt pretty in a very long time.

He knew about her surgery and yet it didn't seem to bother him. He saw her as a woman, as a colleague and, hopefully, a friend. The attention, though, or even the thought that a man—an extremely good-looking man at that—found her attractive was enough to give her self-confidence a much-needed boost.

Of course, it could never mean anything. She could come here to Tarparnii, work, meet new people and flirt with Daniel Tarvon and still return to Australia with her heart firmly in place. Nothing serious could ever happen. Daniel had big decisions to make on his own and she had test results that were still waiting to be confirmed.

She knew she was already attached to Simone

and wondered if she shouldn't pull back a little. She'd only been there for two days and already bonds had formed. That was one thing she hadn't expected at all. It was easy to see that Daniel and Simone were genuine, the real deal, and sharing accommodation with them had afforded her the rare opportunity to see what a real, loving family was like. The family she'd never be able to have. It was a bitter-sweet pill to swallow.

Within a few hours Melora had had her first taste of packing up and moving out for a medical clinic. A large transport truck was loaded with medical supplies as well as canvas tents and other equipment such as poles, ropes and food.

'What happens to Simone when you head out on these clinics?' Melora asked Daniel as she hefted a crate from the hut where they slept and carried it to the transport vehicle.

'She'll spend the day with Nandi—Belhara's wife. Whenever I head out on days away, she barely misses me.' He chuckled but behind his words Melora could see the wheels still turning.

'If you do decide to send her to boarding school, who do you think will take longer to adjust—her or you?' she asked softly, after he'd placed the crate into the truck.

He shrugged. 'More than likely me.' Daniel shook his head and headed back to the supply hut for another crate, and the subject dropped. Soon the PMA team bundled into the rear of another transport truck, which had a canvas roof with a large red cross painted on the side, and the large vehicles rumbled their way out of the village.

'How long will it take to get there?' Melora asked Sue, who was seated next to her on the transport, but it was Daniel who answered. He was sitting opposite her, along with the other members of the team, and yet she seemed to be acutely aware of every move he made. It was wrong. She shouldn't be so aware of him and the fact that she was only brought more consternation and confusion into her life.

'Depending on the number of stops we have to make along the way, about an hour. We need to unpack, set up, do the clinic, pack up and head back to the village all by the time the sun goes down.'

Melora nodded, unable to really look at him except for the odd glance in his direction while he'd been speaking. She'd decided to try and keep her distance from him but was finding it nigh on impossible, especially when the entire medical team consisted of a total of eight people and Daniel was their leader. Professional. She simply needed to be professional and polite, but now that their gaffe about marriage was out in the open it was as though both of them felt self-conscious around the other.

'OK. Thanks,' Melora replied, nodding slowly. 'Just so long as I know.'

'It certainly makes for one very long day,' Sue remarked. 'But so worth it when you see the smile of happiness on a patient's face.'

'This way you'll also get to experience what it's like holding jungle clinics, as we've now come to call them,' Daniel continued, his tone laced with a hint of teasing. 'As opposed to the ones we can do in the clinic building.'

Melora's smile was instant. 'The clinic building with the running water that you love so much?' She couldn't help but meet his gaze, noting that his rich, deep eyes were twinkling with delight.

'Oh, yes, Daniel does love that building.' Sue chuckled. 'We all do.'

'He was stroking the bricks the other day,' Melora felt compelled to point out, teasing him a little. She didn't usually say things like that but in this group of wonderful people she was more relaxed and in teasing Daniel, she hoped it also hid her burgeoning feelings for him...feelings she realised it was going to be difficult to fight, but fight she must.

'I don't blame him,' Sue responded, and as the truck rumbled through the jungle, the entire team joined in the conversation, sharing stories and anecdotes of different scenarios from their pasts. They talked over each other, they laughed, they shared experiences, and Melora couldn't believe how wonderful she felt.

For years she'd been a surgeon attached to the general surgical department, working day in, day out with much the same people, but never had she felt such an instant camaraderie as she did now. Even the brief stopping now and then to go through the necessary checkpoints, Daniel showing their papers before they continued on their way, didn't diminish the level of conversational enjoyment eight medical professionals, all with very different backgrounds, could share.

By the time they arrived at their destination, Melora was filled with an energetic excitement. She followed the necessary directions in helping set up the tents and getting ready for what Daniel called the busiest medical experience of her life.

He leaned in close, his scent tantalising her in that mesmerising way. 'And this is only the beginning.' He flashed her that enigmatic smile of his and then headed off to the well to draw water.

Melora closed her eyes and breathed out. How was she supposed to keep her distance from him when he was so easy to be around?

As she was unpacking the last of the supplies, there was a loud rumbling sound, as though there was thunder above them. The last time she'd checked, there hadn't been a single cloud in the sky.

'What's that noise?' she asked, coming out of the large canvas tent and looking up at the sky.

'It's not thunder, Melora.' Daniel directed her gaze to the surrounding trees and as she watched, several people materialised seemingly from nowhere. 'It's your patients.'

'Sounds like a lot of patients.'

Daniel's answer was to laugh, the rich sound washing over her. 'You said it. Saddle up. It's time to ride the wild clinic,' he called with a joviality Melora found highly infectious. It was clear he loved his work and as the clinic progressed, all of the staff dealing with patient after patient after patient, Melora couldn't believe how much *she* was enjoying herself.

Daniel had arranged for one of the women in the village who had helped them in the past to act as the receptionist-cum-triage nurse while P'Ko-lat worked with Melora in a nursing and translator capacity. It certainly made things easier.

Melora gave injections, checked ears, noses and throats, relocated a shoulder, treated and bandaged sore limbs and even sutured a head wound. Although when a woman was brought to her with severe abdominal pains, it was the first time Melora really wished for state-of-the-art medical equipment to be available at her fingertips. For all of the cases she'd already seen, she'd been able to adapt, to make do or rely on her colleagues to introduce her to an alternate way of doing things. Now, as she felt the woman's abdomen, she knew it could be several different diagnoses and wished she had X-ray facilities.

'Ask Daniel to come through if he's free,' Melora instructed P'Ko-lat. A moment later Daniel came around the cotton sheet partition, erected to afford a certain amount of privacy to their patients. Melora sensed him before she saw him but pushed the thought to the back of her mind.

'Problem?' he asked.

'Just need a second opinion.' She explained her patient's symptoms to him and he, in turn, asked questions in the woman's native language.

'What do you think it is?' he asked.

'Appendicitis, but her symptoms of vomiting, diarrhoea and massive abdominal cramping could be early signs of hernia, bowel obstruction, gastroenteritis, just to name a few.'

'What do you want to do?' Daniel asked.

'Given the lack of means to test and rule things out, and also the fact that she hasn't been able to eat anything for days, I want to open her up. It's the only logical conclusion.'

'Agreed.' Daniel turned to P'Ko-lat. 'Get Belhara in here to give this woman an anaesthetic. Sue can be the surgical nurse and I'll assist Melora.' P'Ko-lat headed off to do his bidding.

'Just like that?' Melora asked. 'Right here, right now, we're going to open her up?' There were no waiting lists. There were no protocols or red tape. There was no theatre!

'*You're* going to open her up. You're the surgeon.'

She glanced at her surroundings, which seemed fine for treating patients but for some strange reason she'd thought they'd take their patient somewhere else to operate. She'd known she'd be doing rough-and-ready medicine when she'd started her research about Tarparnii, but she hadn't fully comprehended the lack of sterile environment. It wasn't the physical act of doing the surgery that was bothering her but the location.

'Daniel! Where's the theatre?'

'Here. There *is* nowhere else to do the surgery. This is the most sterile environment we have and as you can tell by Meimii's blood pressure, we can't wait to take her back to the village.'

'So I operate here?' She trusted Daniel to guide her in what she should do. He'd worked here for so long, he knew the conditions, he knew the risks of infection, but he also knew the risks of not performing the surgery at all.

'You operate. Right here, right now. It's your job to save Meimii's life.'

Melora looked into his eyes, his gorgeous eyes, eyes that she could look into for an exceedingly long time and not get tired of. Eyes that were now reaching out to her, giving her confidence and strength to do the job she'd come there to do. She accepted his strength and squared her shoulders, nodding once in affirmation.

'Then that's exactly what I'll do.'

Daniel had watched the different emotions cross her face and when he saw the one of acceptance, it gave him confidence that she was the right person for the job. She'd fitted into life as a jungle doctor with relative ease, and he felt as though he was watching a butterfly begin to emerge from its cocoon.

Within next to no time Belhara had Meimii anaesthetised. Daniel had ordered someone to draw fresh water from the well, Sue had helped Melora set out the equipment they'd need and to position the operating stretcher for easier access. P'Ko-lat was erecting another set of sheets to provide them with an enclosed environment and then assisted in removing Meimii's clothes.

The ground was dirt, the operating table was a canvas stretcher, the light came from that great big ball of burning gas in the sky called the sun, assisted by a torch one of her colleagues would hold.

Melora had never operated like this before.

After she'd washed and dried her hands, pulled on some gloves and a paper apron to protect her clothes and allowed P'Ko-lat to tie her mask in place, she was physically ready. Mentally, she had reservations but wishing for an X-ray machine or an ultrasound was pointless. She looked directly across her patient to where Daniel stood.

'Ready?' he asked.

Melora swallowed and tried to ignore the flies and other insects that were also in the tent with them. It wasn't her job to shoo them away. It wasn't her job to worry about the conditions. It was her job to save Meimii's life. Daniel had faith in her to perform under such circumstances—she could see it in his brown eyes. This man trusted her, believed in her and, taking strength from him, she nodded.

'Ready.' Holding out her hand to Sue, who was standing beside her, she ordered, 'Scalpel.'

After making a careful and neat incision, Melora started a methodical exploration, deciding to rule out appendicitis first and foremost before checking on other possible reasons for Meimii's pain.

'Looks as though you were right,' Daniel remarked as they looked at the enlarged appendix. 'Good call, Dr Washington.'

'Thank you. Retract, please.'

As she continued to operate, completely in the

zone, Daniel admired her skill. Although he was quite content to be a GP, to be able to assist with surgery and to treat his patients to the best of his ability, he appreciated Melora's skills. She was clear and precise in her instructions so that both he and Sue knew what she needed and when.

At one point she chuckled and he could hear the smile in her words as she spoke. 'I'm used to doing this operation through keyhole surgery. Amazing how dependant we become on technology.'

'Agreed, but we work with what we have and you are doing a mighty fine job, Mel.'

She glanced at him and her eyes twinkled with happiness. 'Thank you.'

Daniel had a receptacle ready to accept the excised organ and once it was out, he checked it as best he could. 'No perforation. How does the site look?'

'Looking good. I think if we'd left Meimii any longer, we'd be dealing with peritonitis.' As the surgery progressed, Melora felt more alive and more invigorated at performing this type of surgery than she had in years. Out here, she could really see how her skills, her knowledge and her expertise really made a difference to people's lives.

After doing a quick exploratory, she was ready to

close, content in the belief that if Meimii followed doctor's orders and took the full course of antibiotics prescribed, she would make a full recovery.

'OK, Belhara. I'm done and you can do your thing,' she finally said once the wound had been sutured closed in layers and then bandaged. As she peeled off her gloves, mask and protective gown, she turned to Daniel, who was doing the same. 'What happens with Meimii's after-care? Does she come back to the clinic with us or—?'

'She'll come back with us.' He nodded. 'Given that you weren't able to perform keyhole surgery and that a laparotomy was required, she's going to need constant care for at least the next two weeks, not to mention ensuring that her wound site stays clear of infection. We can also administer the antibiotics. People in Western society are used to going to the doctor, getting a prescription, having it filled at the pharmacy and then taking a course of antibiotics, knowing the dos and don'ts associated with them.'

'But out here that's not the case?'

'Natural remedies are often used to help with healing and while I am a complete advocate for these, they also have a time and a place. Wherever I can use natural means, I do, but sometimes, such as with Meimii's situation where we've needed to operate in an unsterile environment, it's imperative that she not run the risk of infection.'

'What are some of the natural remedies used? Should I have a crash course in them so I know what to look out for or, alternatively, what treatment to prescribe?'

Daniel couldn't help but be impressed with this woman's attitude and on a whim enveloped her in a big hug. He knew he shouldn't because holding her close was like playing with fire—dangerous—but he hadn't been able to resist. He heard her breathe in sharply at the impromptu contact and quickly eased back before her sweet scent penetrated his defences.

'Thank you, Melora. Thank you for understanding that life here is different. We have so many doctors who come here to help, who hand out Western medicines and think their job is done and dusted. Then we have the doctors who come here, who embrace the wonderful people of Tarparnii, who are interested in the culture, in the festivals, in the beliefs and in the natural medicines that have seen this country through a lot of good and bad times.' Daniel nodded, trying to ignore the way the atmosphere between them had instantly thickened.

He shouldn't have touched her because now he was completely aware of her and itched to haul her close once more. He cleared his throat and took a step back 'I *knew* you were the latter and you've just proved me right.'

'Well…thank you, Daniel.' Feeling self-conscious, Melora found it difficult to meet his gaze. She was still trying to come to terms with the fact that Daniel had just hugged her, held her close, pressed his body to hers. He'd felt warm and solid and given that they'd been out here for quite some time, in hot and humid conditions, her senses had still been teased with that earthy-spicy scent she was coming to equate with him.

'I might just…go and get a drink. A little breather before I jump back into treating the rest of the patients.' And a little breather from being so close to him and having him create absolute havoc with her equilibrium.

'Good idea.' He was about to offer to go with her, to talk about some of the different methods they used in Tarparnii to promote healing, but as she pushed aside the hanging sheet she glanced back at him and the look in her eyes told him she needed some distance.

Had she been aware of the sensations released when he'd hugged her? Was she as affected by him as he was by her? If so, then it would be best for him not to follow her, to respect that she wanted some distance between them.

He knew she was right to keep him at arm's length but he knew himself too well. He was a gung-ho sort of man. When he did something, whether it was driving on mudslides, seeing more patients than he could poke a stick at, or wrestling with a deadly snake, he usually jumped in with both feet, safe in the knowledge that if there were any repercussions, he could think quite quickly on his feet and come through with flying colours.

However, he was starting to question whether that was the case with regard to Melora. She was an amazing surgeon, an incredible woman whose vibrancy had been stripped from her due to cancer, and yet here she was, fighting back, determined to find a new life.

His admiration for her was increasing with every moment he spent in her company and where, in the past, he might have jumped right in to figure out where this admiration might lead him, he now wasn't so sure he'd be able to think quickly enough on his feet.

Putting some distance between them was no doubt a good thing. Working hard to keep their relationship strictly professional was another area where he needed work. After the brief hug he'd just given her, Daniel could clearly acknowledge that he was attracted to Melora Washington.

He'd held her in his arms before, he'd talked to her, he'd offered her comfort, and those memories had played often through his mind during the past few nights since he'd met her. He didn't mind mild flirtations, he didn't mind sharing special moments with incredible women, but the more he got to know Melora, the more he *wanted* to spend more time with her, and it was those sensations that made her very dangerous to be around.

He hadn't planned on meeting Melora. He hadn't planned on being attracted to her. He hadn't planned on his daughter bonding with her so instantly. Melora would be gone soon, back to her world of laparoscopes and X-ray machines. Back to work in a large, impersonal hospital, and he would be here, with Simone.

He hadn't really contemplated remarrying before, his world feeling as though it was already full with work and family and Simone. Now, though, after the silly mix-up with Melora that morning, Daniel wondered if he would indeed get married again. He'd always thought he'd been super-lucky with B'lana. Was it possible for it to happen again?

He and B'lana had been friends for a long time, having had much in common, given they'd both been raised in two cultures, but he'd also been cautious. Having seen his own parents' marriage break down and dwindle to nothing due to cultural differences, he and B'lana had been careful how much time they spent in both England and Tarparnii.

However, if he were to even think about marrying a non-Tarparniian, would she have the same outlook? Would she be willing to spend time in both countries, more in Tarparnii?

He thought about Melora, the woman whose life had changed, the woman who was reaching out for a new life, a new and improved version of herself, and even in the short time she'd been there, he'd started to notice subtle differences.

She no longer tugged and pulled on her oversized shirts, which showed him she wasn't feel as self-conscious as when she'd arrived. She'd embraced the culture with open arms, as though appreciating it for the rare gift it was, and a smile seemed to be on her lips ninety per cent of the time.

Whilst she might love this place now, Australia was her home. His home was here, in Tarparnii, and he knew it was impossible to try and live in two places at the same time. His parents had tried and it hadn't worked, ending in pain for all involved. He and Melora came from different worlds…and never the twain should meet.

CHAPTER SEVEN

For the next few nights they were able to establish a loose routine, where Melora would read a story to Simone at bedtime before Daniel gave his daughter a cuddle. Usually, after that, Simone would drop straight off to sleep, content in the knowledge that she was loved but leaving the two adults to face each other…alone…with no one to act as a buffer.

Tonight, however, as Melora lay next to the child, cuddling her close, Daniel sitting a little further away, listening to her read, Melora couldn't help but be aware of every move he made. She was half concentrating on the story and half on the man who seemed to fill her thoughts during the day and her dreams at night.

When she finished the story, she closed the book and was pleased when Simone snuggled in a bit more. Her arms instantly came around the child, loving the way it felt to hold her close, to offer comfort and love. It was true that this child meant the world to her and Melora had no idea how she was going to leave Simone when her time there was up.

She was breathing in the sweet scent of the four-year-old when Simone spoke her name, tiredness evident in the girl's voice.

'Yes, darling?' Melora answered.

'Why do you feel all different up here?' She eased back and pointed to Melora's chest. 'It's all soft but different on that side. Why?'

Melora couldn't help but tense at the child's words, mortification replacing mellowness. Heat suffused through her and her mouth went dry. Simone had noticed the difference? Melora's heart pounded wildly against her ribs.

'Simone.' There was censure in Daniel's tone as he said the girl's name. 'You shouldn't ask questions like that.'

'But…why?' Simone shifted slightly away from Melora and looked worriedly at her father, completely perplexed by the adults.

'No. No. It's all right, Daniel. It's fine.' Melora reached out for Simone, soothing the child's apprehension and at the same time started to let go of her own. 'You're not to know, sweetheart, and it's a very good question.' Simone went back into Melora's arms, still a little uncertain.

'A while ago I had an operation there. I had a bad lump in my breast and so the doctors needed to take my breast away so that I could live, but I'm fine now.' Even as Melora spoke the words she felt tears prick at her eyes, but this time round they were more as though she was saying goodbye to her old life, rather than for the way her life had been forced to change.

'A bad lump?' Simone asked, yawning and relaxing further.

'That's right, but now that they've removed the bad lump, I'm fine. I'm healthy but it means I need to wear a fake breast—or prosthesis, as they're called—to help me.'

'Oh.' Another yawn. 'So that's why they feel different.'

'Yes.'

'Melora?'

'Mmm?'

'I'm glad they took the bad lump away and that you're fine.'

Melora smiled and dropped a kiss to the little girl's head. 'Me, too.' And she was. For the first time since her surgery Melora was truly pleased that she was indeed fine. If she hadn't found the lump in time, her prognosis could have been a lot worse. As that wasn't the case, she'd been able to receive treatment, to pick up the pieces of her shattered life and to come here, to meet such amazing people and to feel loved by the little girl sleeping in her arms.

Daniel came over and pressed a kiss to Simone's cheek. 'Goodnight, my *Separ*,' he said quietly, before looking across at Melora. 'You handled that very well. I should try to remember to teach my daughter not to ask such difficult questions.'

'I think you'll be fighting a losing battle,' Melora remarked as she shifted the sleeping Simone so the child lay on her frilly pink pillow.

'Probably.' Daniel knelt on the opposite side of Simone, the sleeping child between the two of them as Melora sat up. 'Seriously, though. Are you all right?'

'Medically? Mentally? Physically?'

He smiled. 'All of the above.'

She nodded. 'I'm doing quite well and just now... well, that's the first time I've really been able to articulate, in the simplest way, what happened to me, and do you know what?'

'What?'

'It didn't sound all that scary. I've survived this far.' She smiled and nodded. 'It's nice to be able to say those words out loud and not feel as though my life is crumbling. Finally, I feel as though my feet are on solid ground.' She straightened her shoulders and lifted her head just a little bit higher.

'Mel, that's very good news.'

She swallowed and sighed. 'It is.'

'Well done. That's quite an achievement.'

'Thanks, Daniel. It means a lot to hear you say that.'

The atmosphere between them started to intensify, the awareness building as they sat there, looking at each other, in the diminishing light. She didn't need light, however, to know every contour of Daniel's face, as she'd already memorised each and every one. Being around him, being close to him, being a part of his life, even if it was just for a short period of time, was definitely enough to make her forget the pressures of the past few years and to look forward to whatever her future held.

She licked her lips as she sat there and looked at him, wondering if he was ever going to lose his strong sense of self-control and drag her close, his mouth hungry on hers as they gave into the overwhelming attraction they—

Daniel cleared his throat. 'Excuse me,' he said and without another word he stood and headed out of the shack. Melora closed her eyes as he left, wondering if he'd been able to read the direction of her thoughts. How was she supposed to hide the fact that she was attracted to him when he was so incredible?

The awkwardness between them seemed to stretch even tighter after that night but both of them did their best to ignore it. After the way they'd shared that long and heated look the other morning, plus her gaffe about thinking he'd been proposing marriage to her, something that still caused her cheeks to suffuse with colour every time she thought about it, the atmosphere between them seemed to have shifted.

She'd noticed that while Daniel was still attentive in a professional capacity, he seemed to be putting a bit of distance between them personally. For the first few nights she'd been in Tarparnii they'd both been in the hut at night-time, chatting quietly before dropping off to sleep, Melora, usually exhausted beyond belief. Now, though, after he'd said goodnight to Simone, he would head out of the hut and wouldn't return until much later.

At first she thought he was just giving her some

space, as well as seeing to his duties with the few patients who were in the clinic building, but last night, when he'd come into the hut, she'd asked him if everything was all right.

'Everything's fine, Mel. Sorry. Didn't mean to disturb you.' And with that he'd headed back out of the hut, having barely finished taking his shoes off.

When she'd woken early this morning, he'd been sleeping, facing away from her, his breathing even. Simone had already been awake and about to pounce on her father so Melora had suggested they both tiptoe, albeit not as quietly as Melora had hoped, out of the hut together. If she could entertain Simone in the mornings, thereby giving Daniel a chance to sleep in, she would.

Besides, spending one-on-one time with Simone was like she was being granted a special gift. Knowing the chances of her becoming a mother were quite slim given her increasing age, her lack of husband and all of the health problems she might still need to face…

She stopped her thoughts there, pushing aside the fact that any day now she should be hearing from her specialists to find out whether or not her cancer count was within normal parameters or whether she'd be needing another course of che-motherapy. She'd always known there was a slim possibility of having to cut her trip to Tarparnii short and she'd accepted that fact, but now that she was here, helping out and making a real dif-ference, plus being treated to gorgeous girl cuddles from Simone, Melora really didn't want to leave just yet.

And Daniel? A little voice inside her heart asked the question. If she had to leave tomorrow, wouldn't she miss Daniel? Well, of course she would. He was her colleague and her friend. He'd saved her from a mudslide and a deadly snake, as well as sharing his home with her. Of course she would miss him. She'd miss the way his brown eyes seemed to wash over her, the way his deep rich voice made her body tingle with delight, especially if he was standing close to her...

'Hey, Melora!' Daniel's strong voice cut cross the village clearing and her thoughts. She turned to face him. 'We're all heading down to the water-hole. Come. It'll be great fun.' His smile was warm and sexy and highly inviting and she felt a wave of delight wash over her. Never, in all of her forty-one years, had a man been able to make her blush simply by smiling at her across a village clearing.

He could make the butterflies in her stomach take flight with a simple word, his deep tones resonating through her body and leaving a mass of goose-bumps in their wake.

It was their first day off after days of hectic clinics and all the staff were eager for a bit of rest and relaxation, but at the thought of going to the waterhole Melora swallowed, apprehension and anxiety building within her. While she might be coming to terms with her situation, feeling a little bit more confident in not hiding the fact that she'd had surgery, she also wasn't ready to flaunt her body. She hadn't packed a bathing suit, which had been a deliberate move as she was highly self-conscious about her body at the moment.

Melora nodded and quickly headed into the hut… the hut she shared with Daniel and his daughter. She stood there and closed her eyes, wondering how best to deal with this new turn of events.

'You don't need to swim.'

Melora couldn't help the slightly startled gasp that escaped her lips at the sound of his voice, goose-bumps spreading over her as she opened her eyes and turned to face him.

'Daniel! I…er…didn't hear you come in.'

He smiled at her and her knees started to buckle

from beneath her. She quickly bent down and put her hand on her bag, which was situated next to her bedroll. Looking at him was dangerous. Hearing his sexy voice was dangerous. Standing too close to him was dangerous, and right now, as she was doing all three, she realised she was slap-bang in the middle of a minefield.

'We're almost ready to head to the waterhole but I just wanted to let you know that you don't have to swim if you don't want to.'

'You mean if I feel uncomfortable?'

'Exactly.' He shoved his hands into his pockets and took a step away from her. The woman was kneeling beside her bag, looking up at him with those big honey-coloured eyes of hers as though he'd just granted her the moon. The sun was shining in from behind her, creating a golden, ethereal glow around her. The sight was glorious and intoxicating and he had to force himself to stand firm, not to give in to the need to gently help her to her feet before pulling her into his arms and pressing his mouth firmly to her own.

'Thank you for your concern.'

'I just didn't want you to feel as though there was any pressure. There isn't.'

Melora stood and Daniel took another step back,

almost knocking over a stack of crates filled with medical supplies. He quickly stopped them from toppling over, annoyed with himself for letting this gorgeous woman get to him.

He'd tried over the last few days to put a bit more distance between them, making sure they weren't left alone in the same room or area. Night-times were the worst, especially once Simone dropped off to sleep. The atmosphere between them, particularly as they were both lying down getting ready to sleep, usually became very personal. He would be highly attuned to every breath she breathed, every move she made, every little sigh she uttered as she dropped off to sleep, as though she was sighing out the tension of her day.

He'd often thought about going to her, massaging her shoulders, helping her to unwind, but even the thought of placing his hands onto her skin, of feeling the softness beneath his roughened palms, had been enough to keep him awake most of the night.

So for the past few nights he'd tried his best to remove the temptation and had left the hut, going to the clinic and monitoring the patients, while he'd waited for Melora to fall asleep. Then he'd crept in and eventually settled down enough to drift off into a light sleep.

'I would like to go to the waterhole. We've been so busy since I arrived that I haven't had a chance to see it yet.'

'It's got great style. Amazing shapes and colours,' he said, relaxing a little as he talked of his wonderful land.

'And snakes?'

He paused. 'There *may* be some in the surrounding rocks and trees but they'll keep to themselves. That's their home and we are the intruders. The village policy is to only kill them when they venture too close. A green-belly ringed snake, like the boa constrictor, can kill a small child quite quickly. The children must be protected at all costs.'

'Oh, I completely understand and agree. They are important little cherubs and speaking of that, where is your darling cherub? I thought she'd be in here, getting ready to head to the waterhole?'

'She's already there.'

'I would have thought she'd need to change first?'

Daniel laughed. 'No. She usually swims in her clothes, most of the kids do. Gives the clothes and the kids a bit of bath and within fifteen minutes of getting out they're all dry. It's only you city slickers who feel the need to don a completely different set of clothing in order to enjoy the water.'

Melora smiled at the teasing glint she saw in his eyes before looking down at her khaki shorts and baggy shirt. Instead of allowing it to hang limply at her waist, she'd pulled the edges to one side and tied them into a knot. It meant the shirt was still baggy on top but accentuated her curves. 'Well, I'm going to stay dressed as I am but I will take my sketch pad with me. How's that for different?'

Daniel straightened from where he'd been leaning against the crates. 'I didn't know you could draw. Are you any good?'

'Fair to medium.'

There was a shout outside their hut door from Belhara.

'Are you both ready? We are all leaving.'

'Coming,' Daniel called back, and held the screen door to the hut open for Melora. 'Shall we?'

'Sure.' She picked up her sketch pad and a pencil and headed to the door, determined, as she passed him, not to accidentally touch him. Being that close to Daniel, feeling the warmth radiating out from his body, his breath fanning her cheek… She glanced up at him, just for a split second, and was surprised to find him looking intently back at her.

'Melora.' Her name was a caress upon his lips.

'Daniel?' she breathed, cautious and confused by the veiled desire she saw in his eyes.

'I can't stop thinking about you.' The words were out of his mouth before he could stop them, causing her to gasp in shock before slowly shaking her head.

'Don't. We can't.'

'I know we can't go down that path. I don't want to be attracted to you but...' He stopped and tried again. 'I've tried to fight it but it's there, Melora. Between us. More than friendship.' Neither of them moved, caught in time.

'Daniel.' There was pain in her eyes. 'We can't. *I* can't.'

'I know. We live in different countries, different times, different circumstances.'

'It's not only that...' Melora took a step forward, away from him, heading down the stairs, glad she'd finally managed to get her legs to obey the signals from her brain. 'I'm...uh...waiting.'

Daniel closed the screen door and fell into step beside her as they started walking through the village. 'Waiting for what?'

'Results.'

He stopped short, his eyes wide with concern. He put both hands on her shoulders, turning her to face him. 'You're not OK? The cancer? I thought you'd been given the all-clear? You said the PMA doctors were—'

'Satisfied,' she interrupted. 'The majority of my tests came back before I left but there were a few pathology results that wouldn't be in until later.'

'How much later? When?' There was real concern in his voice and she couldn't believe he cared that much for her. It was odd, especially after Leighton, who had been *supposed* to care about what happened to her, hadn't bothered a jot.

'I'm not sure. Maybe today. Maybe tomorrow. Soon. I'm completely confused as to what day of the week it is.'

'It's Monday.'

'Oh. Then hopefully today.'

'The whole time you've been here, you've had this sort of news hanging over your head?' He gave her a little shake and then dropped his arms, his frustration evident.

'I guess. But—'

'And you didn't think to tell me?'

'I didn't think it was that concerning. Besides,

there's nothing you could have done about it. You can't wave a magic wand and hurry the results through.' She paused. 'Or did you need to know because you're the PMA team leader?'

'No. Not because of that. I'm your friend. Friends help and support each other. I could have…'

'What?'

'Been there for you.'

She visibly relaxed, pleased to know that he really cared about her. 'You have been.'

'Not knowing the results must be incredibly stressful.'

'Yes and no. The results will be in when they're in, and while I'd like to know, I've learned the hard way that stressing about it, fixating on it, obsessing about what it might or might not tell me, isn't any way for me to live, hence why I'm here.' She spread one arm wide, encompassing their present surroundings. 'Tarparnii is full of brilliant distractions.' Such as standing still and losing herself in his eyes. 'I can't even contemplate looking into the future when I'm not all that sure whether I'll need more surgery.' It was why she couldn't get involved with him and Simone.

'Mel.' Daniel shook his head in awe. 'You're an incredible woman. You're much stronger than I think you realise, to speak so calmly, in such a controlled way, when referring to all these things that have happened to you.'

'Believe me. I have enough bad days that sometimes outweigh the good ones.' They started walking again, Melora glad to be on the move. She found it much easier to resist Daniel, to keep her head focused, when she wasn't looking directly at him and when he wasn't looking directly at her.

Thankfully, as they walked along, they discussed their surroundings, passing the tree with three trunks that Daniel had shown her on her very first day here. It seemed so long ago. It felt as though she'd been in Tarparnii for so much longer and she had to admit that in less than a week she felt very different. Her love of medicine, of seeing patients, of helping them had definitely returned, along with the delight at finding so many new friends.

Simone, of course, had been an enormous highlight, the little girl so generous with her affection. Just like her father. Daniel was such a good man and he deserved only the best, which, as far as she was concerned, wasn't her. She would finish up her stint in Tarparnii then return to Australia, where she would do whatever it was the surgeons told her to. If she needed more invasive surgery then that's what she would do. If she didn't, her reconstructive surgery could commence. There was too much going on in her life and she really didn't have any time for her handsome colleague and his daughter…as much as she wished otherwise.

When they arrived at the waterhole, Melora sat on a rock and started to draw, but that was only after she'd recovered from watching Daniel take off his cotton shirt and shoes before jumping into the water to join his friends. Simone laughed and giggled, instantly swimming over to him and placing her arms about his neck so she didn't need to tread water in order to stay afloat. Melora was surprised at what good swimmers the children were, especially Simone.

When, after a while, Daniel clambered onto the rocks before heading in her direction, she tried so hard not to notice his incredible body, so firm and dark and gorgeous. She was a doctor, a surgeon, for heaven's sake. She'd seen naked chests before but…never like this!

Small, fine droplets of water clung to his dark skin and the smattering of dark, curly hair that spread down towards his shorts, which he wore low on his hips, glistened in the sunlight. She licked her lips, idly wondering what it would be like to brush her fingers across his skin, to feel the heat radiating from those perfectly sculpted arms of his, to have his mouth pressed to hers, robbing her of breath as he took her to new heights, to kiss—

'You shouldn't look at me like that, Melora.' His tone was deep and intimate so that only she could hear. He settled himself on a rock next to her and propped himself up on one elbow as their gazes met. She saw the intensity in his eyes and felt a mass of tingles flood her body.

'Sorry.' She immediately looked away, swallowing over her embarrassment.

'Don't be. I'm not saying I don't like it—I do, I *really* do—but we're friends and colleagues. I'd hate there to be animosity between us.'

He had to admit that he was still a little hurt that she hadn't told him about her situation sooner. Perhaps not at first but over the past few days they'd most certainly become closer.

Then again, he'd already gathered that Melora was a very private person and as he'd been raised in and now lived in a small Tarparniian community, where everybody knew everyone's business, he often forgot that new PMA doctors tended not to live by those same values.

'Festering is not good for the soul,' his mother

had often said, and he'd heard Meeree say the same sort of thing. Right now, though, Daniel was definitely trying to keep the way Melora made him feel close to his chest. It wasn't festering, per se, but it also wasn't his usual modus operandi. Then again, he'd never been attracted to another woman since B'lana's death so he was definitely in uncharted territory.

The fact that he could still sense that Melora was uncomfortable with the discussion they'd just had was evident so he decided to change the subject. 'Do you mind if I take a look at your drawings?'

Melora still held her sketch pad in her hands and although she was hesitant to show him, she decided it was better to focus on her sketches rather than how close his body was to her own. She flicked over a page and showed him the brief drawings she'd made of him and his friends in the waterhole.

'Wow. These are really good, Melora.' He sat up and gave them his full attention. 'How long have you been drawing?'

'Not long. I started as a means of relieving boredom when I was stuck in hospital. I went from being a hectic surgeon with waiting lists here and there to having a lot of free time. I'd always enjoyed art back in high school so decided to give it another go. The psychologist I saw also said it would be very therapeutic.'

'And has it been?'

'Yes. When my engagement ended, I started to paint a lot of dark, night scenes. Angry clouds, lightning, a lot of destruction.'

'You were engaged?' Daniel tried to make the question sound as disinterested as he could but he knew he'd failed. Again it only reiterated just how much he didn't know about her.

'Yes.' Melora sighed. 'Leighton was Head of Surgery. When we became engaged it was touted as being the marriage of the hospital…only the marriage part never eventuated.'

'Why not?' He pushed aside any feelings of jealous and instant dislike he felt for the unknown Leighton, telling himself he needed to be a supportive friend, for Melora's sake.

'We were both so busy. Our schedules regularly conflicted and whenever Leighton tried to pin me down to a date, something always cropped up. A conference, a research programme, a journal article deadline.'

'You're published?'

'A bit.'

'You're lying. That much I can tell,' Daniel said turning his head to look at her for a moment before deciding it was too dangerous to gaze at her soft, supple skin not too far away from him.

'A few articles over the years. I've done a lot of research and publishing those findings is part and parcel of the whole thing. My dance card, as they say, was completely full.' She sighed. 'So, as it turns out, was Leighton's. He'd been having multiple affairs with different women behind my back.'

Daniel growled at this news, furious with the disgusting Leighton for treating a woman such as Melora with so much contempt. 'When did you find out?'

'When he told me.'

'He confessed?'

'In a way.' Her voice had thickened with emotion and he could hear the pain in her words. 'Two days after my mastectomy surgery. He said it would be best if we called off the engagement, that I'd no doubt want to concentrate on my recovery rather than having to worry about planning a wedding. He then went on to say that he'd met someone else and it would be better for the entire general surgical department if we simply stayed colleagues.'

'He said that? Two days after you'd had major surgery?'

'Among other things.'

Daniel propped himself up on his elbow and looked down into her face. She had her eyes closed, tiny tears trembling on her lashes as she worked hard to control her emotions. No wonder she had self-confidence issues. This Leighton chap, along with the cancer, had destroyed her.

'Once our engagement was officially over, all the stories about his affairs came pouring out, everyone telling me I was too good for him.'

'You are. You *are* too good for him.' Daniel's tone was filled with vehemence. 'A woman like you deserves to be loved with honour, to be cherished with heart-felt desire and to be protected with firm strength.' He reached out and tenderly brushed the tears from her eyes with his thumb.

Melora opened her eyes and stared into Daniel's face. His hand caressed her cheek, the touch soft and tender. She swallowed, her breathing intensifying again, but this time it was due to desire rather than anger at her past.

He was close, his breath mixing with hers. Her heart pounded wildly against her chest and she wondered if he could hear it, it was so loud.

'You're a strong, independent woman, Melora Washington.' His words were barely a whisper, touching her deep down inside. 'I wonder if *you* know just how strong you really are.' He brushed his thumb across her lips and they parted with anticipatory longing. Her breathing was erratic, her mind puzzled at hearing a man speak so highly of her. No man had *ever* upheld her, hence why she'd always fought for what she'd wanted.

'Daniel.' His name came from her lips mixed with repressed passion and confusion. 'What's happening?'

'I don't know,' he answered truthfully. 'Our lives have collided, Mel. Slammed into each other with a resounding *thwack*.' His words were whispered as he edged closer. 'I have no idea what it means but it's becoming more and more difficult for me to deny how you make me feel.'

'Oh...' The word was released on a trembling breath and she swallowed again as Daniel continued to move nearer, her gaze flicking between his mouth and his eyes, her mind spinning so fast as she tried to make some sort of sense out of what was happening.

He was going to kiss her! She could sense it. She could feel it and she wasn't at all sure what she should do about it—if anything. The fact that Daniel admitted to finding her attractive, that he was interested in her, that he thought her a strong, intelligent woman was already more than she'd ever dreamed of…but the truth of the matter was they came from different worlds and really shouldn't… follow through…on…

Her mind stopped working, stopped processing, stopped trying to make any sort of sense of what was happening between them, simply because all she could think about was his mouth finally touching hers.

CHAPTER EIGHT

'DAD-DYY. Mel-ora.' Simone's voice penetrated Daniel's mind and without shifting his body, still remaining close to Melora's delicious mouth, his thoughts still firmly directed towards following through on his desire to kiss her, he slightly turned his head to the side. Melora did the same, their cheekbones resting together as they looked over to where Simone was trying to get their attention.

The child had climbed onto a rock and was about to jump into the water, her friends waiting below, encouraging her. The rock, however, was one of the higher ones and Daniel's parental alarm instantly started ringing in loud warning tones.

'It's too high,' Melora whispered, both of them moving, rising to their feet.

'It's too high,' Daniel called a moment later. 'Simone. Get down.' Daniel looked around them, realising that Belhara was already out of the water and was heading around on the rocks to get to the little girl.

Simone wiggled her hips and clapped her hands, her wet blonde hair swishing from side to side. The shorts and T-shirt she wore were wet and dripping down onto her bare feet, causing the rock she was standing on to become dangerously slippery. 'I'm nearly five,' she told her father.

'It's too high,' Melora called, her heart—where it had been pounding wildly in sensual anticipation—now thumping wildly with fear and trepidation.

'*Separ*,' Daniel coaxed in a firm but gentle tone. 'It's too high. Turn around and climb back down. When you're ten, then you will be old enough to—'

'I'm old enough now,' she protested illogically, and shifted closer to the edge.

Melora stood, her hands clasped tightly to her chest, feeling helpless and inadequate, willing the child to be sensible, to listen to her father.

'Simone.' There was now a stern warning in Daniel's tone and Simone stopped and looked at him, realising she was making her beloved daddy angry. Melora watched as the visual stand-off between father and headstrong daughter continued as they held each other's gaze. There was nothing she could do and she felt so useless.

She wasn't the little girl's mother but she most

certainly felt like it. The love, the need to protect, the powerful surges of wanting to keep the gorgeous girl close to her for the rest of her life—it was all there, and where she'd been telling herself not to become too involved in these people's lives, she was starting to realise that it might actually be too late.

Belhara had climbed the rocks and was now within reaching distance of Simone. Within another moment he would be able to snake out his arm and put it around her little waist, hauling the child back to safety. Melora's throat was dry, her eyes wide with concern, her heart filled with a silent prayer.

The children in the water below, the ones who had been encouraging Simone, probably daring Simone to jump, were now silent, being told by one of the other parents to come out of the water.

Belhara was almost there. His arm almost touching her but the last thing any of them wanted was to spook the child, who was now crying.

'I'm sorry, Daddy.' Where there had been courage in her tone before, it had now changed to trembling fear and it was as though she was glued to the spot, unable to move.

'It's all right, *Separ.*' Daniel, who was now

standing at the edge of the waterhole, looking pleadingly up at his daughter, made sure his tone held no censure. 'Turn around slowly. Carefully. Go with Belhara.'

As Daniel spoke, Belhara's arm touched Simone, startling the child. She screamed in fright and shifted away but as she did so, her little feet slipped on the rock and within another second there was a sickening thud—the sound of bone connecting with something hard—before the child dropped into the water. Had she just hit her head? Had that sound been her head hitting against the slippery rock?

'No!' Melora hadn't realised the scream had come from her and she made her way towards the water's edge, heart pounding fiercely against her chest, tears welling in her eyes. She looked around for Daniel but couldn't see him, realising a split second later that he'd already dived into the water to rescue his daughter.

'Oh, God. Please let her be OK,' Melora prayed, clutching her hands to her chest, realising belatedly that she was trembling in fear. She'd never been this frightened, this concerned, this worried before. Not when she'd been diagnosed with breast cancer, not when she'd had surgery, not even when

Leighton had broken their engagement, leaving her to face her recovery all alone.

No. Nothing compared with the pain a parent would feel if *anything* bad happened to their child, and her heart ached for Daniel. It seemed like hours ticked by while she waited for the two of them to surface, even though it was only a matter of seconds.

The instant they broke through the water's surface, Simone's loud, wailing cries filled the air, and Melora couldn't believe the relief which flooded over her. Her knees buckled beneath her and she landed in the shallows of the water, unable to move, watching as Daniel swam towards her, Simone crying loudly.

When they were closer, she held out her hands and Daniel instantly passed Simone to her. Melora pressed kisses to the child's head, cradling her close. Simone was still crying, hopefully more through fear than pain.

'It's OK. It's OK,' she soothed, rocking back and forth, her arms secure around the child. Daniel had pulled himself next to them and leaned over Simone.

'Let me take a look. Does it hurt? Where does it hurt, baby? Show Daddy.'

Simone nodded her little head and pointed to her arm which, now that they had the opportunity to look at her properly, Melora realised, was hanging limply at a very wrong angle. Daniel was touching it gently but even then Simone was whimpering.

'Feels fractured. We need to get her back to the clinic and have Keith take a look at it,' he murmured close to her ear, and although his words were clinical, Melora could hear the veiled panic.

'She'll be fine, Daniel,' she reassured him. 'You had her out of the water so fast, even though it felt like an eternity. You were there. You were looking after her.'

'I should have done more. I should have been watching her. Playing with her in the water. Protecting her, rather than thinking only of myself. She's my child. My responsibility,' he returned, his words crisp as he stood and lifted Simone from Melora's arms. The child whimpered again and Daniel cradled her close. 'Shh. It's fine. Daddy's got you. Daddy's going to fix you and make it all better.'

Melora looked at him as she managed to stand up, reaching out a hand to brush some hair back from Simone's face. His face was an emotionless mask, his eyes dull yet filled with pain. 'I should have been with her.' Daniel edged away, putting some distance between them, and Melora dropped her hand back to her side, feeling as though she'd just been slapped.

'I need to get her to the clinic,' he said, and without another word turned and started to make his way expertly over the rocks, his daughter held protectively in his arms. Melora knew he was concerned, she understood that he was worried about Simone—so was she—but she hadn't missed the way Daniel was blaming himself for the accident. If he hadn't been paying attention to her, if he'd been watching his daughter more closely, the accident might never have happened.

She stood in the shallows of the water, watching them walk away, feeling lonely and bereft. She wasn't Simone's mother, she wasn't even a member of Daniel's extended Tarparniian family. She was just a doctor who had come to help out for a while. Someone who would leave soon, who would return to Australia and probably never see either one of them again.

At that thought, at the realisation that she could face the rest of her life without either Daniel or Simone, Melora's heart contracted with a new sort of pain. It was powerful and intense and one she'd never felt before. She'd survived cancer, she'd survived the messy break-up with Leighton, but the thought of surviving the rest of her life without Simone and Daniel made her heart break.

She needed to do something. She couldn't just stand there and watch two people that she cared about most in this world just walk away from her, especially when one of them was hurt! She'd felt helpless and alone when she'd made the decision to come to Tarparnii and on her arrival here she'd learned that the main thing about these villages was a sense of community. J'tana had been cared for by her sister and her mother during the delivery of her first child. Meeree and Jalak offered friendship and family to all of the people who came to their village, whether to receive treatment from the doctors, or the doctors coming from overseas to help out.

Friendship. Family. Community.

That's what *she* had found, that's what Daniel and Simone had helped her to feel, and after quickly scooping up her sketch pad she hurried after them, eager to offer her services and support in any way she could. Daniel might brush her aside, might hold her at arm's length because he was mad at himself, but that wouldn't stop her from giving to him, from caring for him, from showing him that he was important to her.

Although she didn't have her final tests results in yet, although she would be leaving this glorious place soon to return to Australia, although she wasn't sure how her affections would be received, she had to take this chance. She had to show Daniel that she cared.

Even though she hurried, picking her way through the jungle, on the path, past the three-trunked tree, Melora still didn't manage to catch up with them, and when she entered the clinic, the sounds of Simone crying tore at her heart. She entered the examination area where Keith was having a look at Simone's arm. Daniel was sitting on the examination bed holding Simone in his arms, his emotionless mask still in place.

Daniel didn't even glance her way when she came in, his attention focused on what was happening to his little girl. It was as though the doctor in him had disappeared, leaving a nervous and worried father behind.

'We'll get you some medicine, Simone,' Keith was saying to the little girl. 'That will make you feel better and take away that nasty pain.' Keith looked at Daniel. 'She's not allergic to anything is she? Tarvon?'

Daniel didn't answer and Keith looked over at Melora, concern on his face. Melora nodded and instantly went to Daniel's side.

'Hey.' She put her hand on his shoulder, reassuring and comforting this man who had come to mean so much to her in such a small amount of time. Slowly he turned his head to look at her and Melora smiled. 'Everything's going to be just fine, Daniel.'

Simone whimpered in his arms and he winced as though he was the one who was in agony. 'Daniel, is she allergic to anything?'

He shrugged. 'I don't know. She's never had anything wrong with her before.'

Keith nodded and crossed to the cupboard, drawing up an injection of Midazolam. Melora looked down at the little girl, still held safely in her father's loving arms. 'Hi, sweetie.'

Simone sniffed and her words were full of misery. 'I hurt my arm, Melora.'

'I know, but Keith is going to make it all better. You'll be just fine.' While Melora spoke, she dropped her hand from Daniel's shoulder, as it would be all too easy to leave it there. Given the emergency, he hadn't had time to don his shirt, and being this close to his torso, to his smooth warm flesh wasn't helping her to keep focused.

Right now, Daniel needed friends around him and she wanted to tell him that she was there for him, in whatever capacity he required. She wanted to tell him that it wasn't his fault that his daughter had had the accident, that it had been circumstantial. She wanted to tell him just how much he'd come to mean to her and how it was becoming increasingly difficult for her to stop wanting to be close to him.

But she didn't. Now was neither the time nor the place.

Keith administered the anaesthetic and Simone soon became sleepy, dozing off. 'You can put her down now, Tarvon. From what I can see, it appears to be a clean break, nothing a quick re-set and a cast won't fix.'

There was no movement. Daniel still sat there, his sleeping daughter in his arms. Keith once more looked at Melora. 'Here, Daniel.' She gently put her hands at his waist and urged him to stand up. 'Pop Simone on the bed and you and I can head out for some fresh air.'

Daniel lifted his gaze from his daughter and

once more looked at Melora before nodding. 'Yes. Yes. OK. Good.' Tenderly, he placed his daughter on the examination table. Keith put his hand onto Daniel's shoulder.

'Trust me, buddy. I'll be looking after her as though she were one of my own.'

'Thank you.' Daniel allowed Melora to lead him from the room and once they were outside the clinic building, he leaned against the warm bricks and raked his hands through his now dry hair. 'I shouldn't have taken my eyes off her. How could I have been so selfish?'

'It was an accident, Daniel. They do happen and she's going to be fine. Keith is a brilliant ortho-paedic surgeon. We both know that and he'll fix her up as good as new.'

Daniel looked at her. 'I know. I trust Keith. I was just so…caught up…in…you and how you make me feel and…' He stopped and shook his head. Melora could see sadness in his eyes and her heart went out to him. 'Anything could have happened to her. She could have hit her head or fallen into the water at a bad angle and split her skin, she could have really done some damage and—'

'Shh.' Melora couldn't bear his words, his an-guish any more, and put her finger over his mouth to stop him talking. He put his hand around her wrist and held it. 'She didn't, Daniel. You can't watch her twenty-four hours a day. We head off on clinics to other villages and she's always safe here in the village with the rest of your people.'

'But I promised B'lana I'd keep her safe.'

'And you do. You're a good father, Daniel.' Her words were earnest, imploring, desperate to get through to him. 'Don't go beating yourself up because that's just a waste of energy and right now you're better off expending that energy in being with Simone. She needs her happy, big, strong, protective daddy, which is exactly what you are.'

He was still holding her wrist, his thumb gently caressing the lower part of her palm as she spoke. It was difficult to concentrate, difficult to remember she was supposed to be helping him when all she wanted was to kiss him.

'You're right.'

She smiled at that. 'Words every woman wants to hear.'

Daniel gave a little tug on her wrist, drawing her closer. She went.

'I apologise if I snapped at you earlier.'

'Don't worry about it. You were concerned for Simone. I understand.'

'Mel…' He brought her hand to his lips and pressed a long and tender kiss to her soft skin. Melora closed her eyes for a second, committing the touch to memory because when she looked at him again, there was sorrow in his beautiful brown eyes.

'We can't do this.' The words were soft, sweet and sad. 'Simone is my world. She's my everything.'

'As she should be.'

'I've never been this interested in a woman since B'lana's death and I want you to know that you are important to me but right now I have to put Simone first.'

'Of course you do.' Melora swallowed over the dryness in her throat and gently eased back from him. Daniel reluctantly let go of her hand and as he did she was astonished to find there were tears pricking behind her eyes. She forced a smile and ignored the pain around her heart. 'I'm, uh…going to go and get a drink.'

Biting her lip in an effort to control the trembling sadness wrenching out from her, she knew the sooner she had some space from him, the sooner she'd be able to get herself under control. Hearing him say that he was interested in her had been incredible and then to hear, in the same breath, that he couldn't do anything about it, was playing over and over in her mind.

'Sure.' Daniel pushed his hands through his hair and nodded, feeling hollow as he watched her go. When he'd asked her to come to the waterhole with them, he'd had no idea that things would escalate so quickly. He'd been sidetracked from watching Simone by the stunningly beautiful Melora, her golden hair shining brightly in the sun. He'd been looking at her drawings, wanting to get close to her, wanting to touch her, wanting to kiss her.

The fact that he was even interested in another woman, had wanted to pursue her, was a miracle in itself because after B'lana's death, although she'd told him to find someone else, he'd never thought he'd ever again meet anyone who he connected with so completely. Meeting Melora had proved him wrong and he'd allowed himself to be sidetracked from his main responsibility—his daughter.

Simone was his world and he'd been right to put the brakes on anything else that might have happened between Melora and himself. Simone needed him now and it would be selfish of him to focus on himself, on the rapidly increasing feelings he felt for his newest colleague.

'Tarvon?'

Daniel looked around as someone called his name, to see Jalak headed in his direction. 'She's fine,' Daniel said quickly. 'Broken arm. Keith's fixing her up now.'

Jalak nodded and smiled. 'Simone will be running around sooner than you realise.' Jalak tapped the side of his head. 'It is the father who will have the lasting image. Children bounce and forget. As parents we do not.'

'True.'

'I am also wanting Melora. You have seen her? There is a call on the satellite phone for her.'

'That must be about her results,' Daniel said, more to himself than to Jalak. 'She's in the food hut. I'll get her.' He knew she wouldn't want to be alone when she found out the results. It must have been nerve-racking for her to come here without knowing the outcome of her final tests and yet, like the strong, independent woman she was, she'd still come.

He sincerely hoped it was good news and just as he headed off to the food hut, Keith came out of the clinic. 'Ah…just the man I was looking for. Break's set, Cast's in place and she's about to wake up.'

Daniel looked from Keith to the food hut where he knew Melora was, and back again.

'Go to your child,' Jalak encouraged. 'I will tell Melora of the call.'

And once more Daniel realised that now was not the right time in his life to be moving on, to be trying something new with an amazing woman. He nodded and headed into the clinic. It was time for him to look after his baby girl.

Later, after night had fallen, Melora stopped by the clinic to check on Simone. The child was sitting up in one of the hospital beds, chatting brightly to anyone who would listen. Her plastered arm was resting on a large blanket in front of her as though it was her pride and joy.

'Hello, gorgeous girl.' Melora knelt down beside the bed and was treated to a huge one-armed hug from Simone.

'Look at this, Melora. Look at my cast. I have a cast and Daddy says that he'll find me a big pen and people can write their names on it and it has to stay on for three weeks and Keith said I was very lucky and that 'cos my arm is only four-and-three-quarters, nearly five years old it will be all better really soon and Sue brought me some fresh fruit from the tree and Bel comes and checks on me and takes my temperature and I get to sleep here tonight!'

Melora laughed at the run of constant chatter. 'Wow. That's…really a lot of things happening.'

'And Daddy's going to sleep here too but he's not allowed to use one of the beds because they're for the sick people so he's gone to get his sleeping mat from our hut and…ooh, you could get your sleeping mat and come on the other side and we can *all* sleep in the clinic.' Her eyes were wide and she scrunched her shoulders up with delighted excitement. 'I've *never* slept in here before. I wanted to but Daddy said no and that only sick people got to sleep here but I'm sick now and so I get to stay here but Daddy said just for tonight.'

'Yes. He's quite right. One night should be just the right amount to help make you better.' Before Melora had finished speaking, Daniel walked in, his sleeping mat and blankets rolled up beneath his arm. He'd also donned a shirt so his naked chest wasn't causing her as much havoc as it had before. He still looked incredible, though.

'Daddy! Melora's going to sleep here, too. You on one side and Melora on the other and me in the middle. Just like all the time in our hut,' Simone informed him before Melora could say anything.

'Actually, I don't know if there would be enough room,' Daniel said quickly. 'We need to make sure that Bel can get close to your clinic bed to take your temperature and look after you during the night.'

Melora frowned. She'd already been going to refuse the little girl's offer but to have Daniel do it for her felt like another slap in the face. 'Daddy's right and, besides, it will be a great adventure for the two of you to have.'

Simone's bottom lip came out, her brown eyes mimicking those of a sad puppy. 'But I want you to be here. You're like the mummy and Daddy's like the daddy and then we can all stay together. Family.'

Tears of delight instantly sprang into Melora's eyes at Simone's words. *You're like the mummy.* She smiled but her sadness was evident. 'You and Daddy stay here tonight and then you'll have lots of exciting news to tell me in the morning. OK?'

She couldn't look at Daniel. Couldn't even bring herself to glance in his direction. She had no idea how he'd coped with Simone's declaration at how she saw the three of them but as he'd said outside not a few hours before, he needed to focus on Simone. It was true and right and after she kissed the child, she headed out of the clinic.

She'd not made it halfway across the village clearing when she heard Daniel call her name. She turned and clasped her hands together in front of her.

'Uh…sorry to bother you, but Jalak mentioned earlier that you'd received a call on the satellite phone.'

'Yes.'

'Was it your results?'

'Yes.'

She wasn't making this easy for him but then again why should she? He'd all but pushed her aside, telling her that he had feelings for her but wasn't going to do anything about it. In a few more days she would be back in Australia and out of his life. Even though he didn't like it, it was the only way for things to be.

'Good news?'

'Yes.' Her smile was watery but she swallowed over the lump in her throat. 'Everything's fine. I am now officially cancer free. My oncologist doesn't want to see me for another twelve months.'

'Oh, Mel, that's brilliant.' He wanted to rush

towards her, take her in his arms, swing her around in a large circle before hauling her close and showing her just how happy he was by kissing her deeply, passionately, completely. Instead, he clenched his jaw and crossed his arms firmly over his chest. 'Congratulations.'

'Thanks.'

Both of them stood there. Silent. Uncomfortable. Painfully aware of each other but unable to do anything about it.

What she really wanted was for him to close the distance between them, tell her that he was wildly ecstatic at her good news and now that she no longer had an axe swinging over her head, he wanted her to stay permanently in Tarparnii, to be with him and Simone, and that she really should go and get her sleeping mat so they could all bunk down in the clinic and have a fantastic time together…as a family.

He didn't.

What he really wanted was for her to run towards him and throw herself into his wide-open arms, telling him that she wanted to stay in Tarparnii, that she loved it here and that her life had become meaningless without him and Simone.

She didn't.

Silence reigned.

'Well…goodnight,' she finally ventured.

'Have a good sleep.'

'You, too. I hope Simone settles down, she's still very hyped.'

'Side-effect of the pain medication Keith has her on.'

'Or is it more the fact that she's super-excited to sleep in the clinic?'

He nodded slowly. 'Good point.'

Silence. Insects chirruped around them.

'Goodnight,' she said again and before anything else was said or done she turned her back to him and walked calmly to the hut—*his* hut—where she unrolled her sleeping mat, prepared for bed and lay down.

All alone.

Again.

CHAPTER NINE

THE next morning Melora woke early. When she opened her eyes she saw no Simone and no Daniel. Just crates of supplies.

It was ridiculous to feel so alone, given that in Australia she lived on her own. Every morning she would wake to the décor of her apartment, alone in her bed, and not have any problems getting on with her day. Now, though, even though the birds were chirping outside, she missed Simone, missed spending those early morning hours with the gorgeous girl. She missed hearing Daniel's steady breathing as he caught up on his sleep.

Was this what it was going to be like when she returned home? When she flew back to Australia in a week's time? She'd come to Tarparnii to stretch her wings, to try new experiences, and she had. However, she hadn't expected to leave feeling more alone than when she'd arrived.

She rolled over onto her stomach and closed her eyes, not wanting to think about it. Daniel and

Simone. Having them around, sharing this hut with them had only succeeded in showing her how wonderful it would be to become part of their family.

The three of them. A family. Together. Supporting. Loving.

'No.' She couldn't think like that. Daniel had made it clear yesterday that there was no place in his life for her and she needed to respect his decision. Even when he'd come to the hut last night to collect Simone's frilly, pink pillow for her to sleep with, Melora's hopes had skyrocketed, hoping, for one brief instant, that he'd come to the hut to tell her he was wrong and that she really should come and join them in the clinic rather than being here by herself.

He'd come into the hut, politely apologised for disturbing her, collected the pillow and called a quick goodnight before leaving, and her hopes had plummeted into the pit of despair.

He wasn't a part of her life. He was just a colleague she was working with for one more week and most of that week would be spent in a different village. They were due to leave in a couple of days' time to head further south to spend the rest of the week in the village of Daniel's mother. From there,

Melora, Sue and Keith were to leave, their time in Tarparnii coming to an end. While Melora was intrigued to meet Daniel's mother, she wasn't looking forward to leaving Meeree and Jalak. Everyone here had been so incredibly welcoming and so incredibly supportive.

She sighed. Lying there, doing nothing except working herself up into a tizz, wasn't going to accomplish anything. She needed to get up and go and see Simone, to check on how the child had slept and how she was feeling. Of course, Melora had other patients to check on, such as Meimii and J'tana—who had decided to head back to her village—but it was the thought of seeing Simone that prompted Melora to actually get up and get her day started.

Before she even stepped foot inside the clinic, she heard Simone laughing and her heart instantly relaxed. The girl was happy. That meant a lot.

'Melora!' Simone almost squealed her name as Melora walked into the room, the little girl running over. Melora picked the child up and held her close.

'J'tana let me have a careful hold of J'torek and I put my frilly pink pillow over my cast arm and then Bel put J'torek in my arms and I had a cuddle but then he started to cry and so now J'tana has to give him mother's milk but I was very careful with him, wasn't I, J'tana?' Simone switched between Tarparnese and English with fluidity, depending on who she was talking to.

'I'm sure you were.' Melora smiled at J'tana and Meimii, both of whom were in their beds, talking to each other while J'tana fed her son. However, there was no sign of Daniel. 'Where's your dad?' Melora asked, trying to make the question sound as natural as possible.

'He's sleeping,' came the deep, muffled reply from somewhere on the floor beside Simone's bed. Melora smiled at the grumpy, exhausted tone of his voice. She looked at Bel, who was getting ready to do Meimii's observations.

'Simone took a while to settle last night. Lots of excitement,' the Tarparniian nurse informed her.

'Ahh. Well, how about we give Daddy the chance to have a bit of a rest? We can go to the food hut, have breakfast and read a book,' Melora suggested to the little girl.

'Like we do *every* morning?' Simone's excitement was boundless.

'Yes.'

'Can we still do that with my arm all broken?'

'Of course we can.'

'Yay!' Simone hugged Melora close with her good arm.

'We'll leave you in peace,' Melora said, and with great delight she and Simone went to the food hut. She would miss this little girl so much, holding her, cuddling her, sharing with her. She decided it was very important that she make as many memories as she could, to store all of these special moments away, because she knew that on her return to Australia she would experience an emptiness such as she'd never felt before. That would be when she'd need these memories, of Simone, of the whole village, but mostly of Daniel, to keep her warm on the long lonely nights.

As the day progressed, Simone bounced back to her normal self and apart from the cast on her arm it was as though nothing bad had ever happened. Daniel, however, was another story. He remained polite and professional towards her but she also noticed that he seemed preoccupied.

Over the next couple of days he became even more withdrawn, not only from her but from everyone. He spent every free moment he wasn't working with Simone, monitoring her, watching her, caring for her. Melora was becoming increasingly concerned and on the morning when they were due to travel to his mother's village she noted that he didn't even bother sleeping.

With Simone sound asleep beside her, Melora tossed and turned but her concern for Daniel, from the way he was only focusing on work and his daughter, was robbing her of sleep. Sighing, she flicked back her covers and pulled on a long cardigan, which covered her summer pyjamas. With bare feet she padded through the hut and on opening the screen door found Daniel sitting on the top step of the hut, looking up at the sky.

'Hi,' she said, coming to sit beside him.

'Mel? What's wrong? Is it Simone? Is she all right?' He stood and was about to head into the hut when she stopped him.

'She's fine, Daniel. She's sleeping…snoring, actually.'

Daniel opened the door of the hut to check for himself and returned a second later, coming down the stairs, needing some distance from where Melora sat. 'Did she wake you? She can snore pretty loud sometimes, especially for someone so small.'

'No. She didn't wake me. I was…uh…concerned about you.'

'Me?' His eyebrows hit his hairline.

'Yes, you. Am I not allowed to be concerned about you?'

'Er…I don't know.' He shoved his hands into the pockets of his shorts to stop himself from touching her, hauling her close into his arms.

'Why don't you come and sit down and we can talk?'

Daniel remained where he was, at the bottom of the steps, looking at her. So close, yet so far. 'I don't know if that's a good idea. No offence, Melora, but being around you is difficult. You're beautiful and caring and wonderful and you smell so good all the time.' He took a hand from his pocket and raked it through his long hair. He hadn't shaved for a few days so his rugged stubble back in place, making him look just as he had when they'd first met—dangerously sexy.

'Oh!' Melora's eyes widened at his frank and honest words. 'Uh…sorry…but, hey, you're one to talk. Don't you think I have trouble being around you? Don't you realise that when you stand there with your hair loose and your arm muscles almost bursting out of your misbuttoned shirt and…and that sexy look in your eyes, as it is right now, that *I* have trouble resisting you?'

'Oh. I…uh…didn't realise.'

'This isn't all one-sided, you know. I know you told me that you couldn't get involved and I understand that. I appreciate that fact and I also know it doesn't change the way we may feel about each other, but that's not why I wanted to talk to you.'

'It isn't?'

'No. I wanted to ask you if you'd come to any decisions about Simone's education.'

'Why would you ask that?'

'Because you've been very preoccupied of late, almost to the point of being withdrawn, and I wondered if Simone's accident had triggered your deeper thought processes.'

'That's very perceptive of you. Have you been taking lessons from Meeree?'

She smiled. 'No. It's actually more like a lucky guess.'

'Well, it's a good one.' He exhaled harshly then shook his head. 'I feel as though my head is going to explode. My thoughts keep going round and round.'

'About whether to send her to boarding school?'

'No. I've come to a decision on that front. She's not going.' His words were vehement. 'After her accident, I realised that I couldn't parcel her off, send her overseas to another country far, far away while I stay here to help out with my people. I will not leave my daughter to be raised by strangers and it's better for both of us if she stays here.'

Melora nodded. 'Decision reached.'

'Yes.' He frowned when she remained silent. 'You're not going to talk me out of it?'

'Why should I? She's your daughter, your responsibility, and you know what's best for her. You know she'll get a different education here but perhaps that's all she needs. Her community is here, she's happy, you're happy. Academic excellence isn't the be-all and end-all in life.'

'Yes. Exactly.'

'So why aren't you happy with your decision?'

'What makes you think that?'

'Daniel, for the past few days you've been so preoccupied, so withdrawn, always with that same concerned look on your face that you have right now, that if you had truly made the right decision, you'd be feeling a lot more at peace.'

He breathed in deep and shook his head slowly. 'How do you do that?'

'Do what?'

'Appear to know me better than I know myself.'

Melora shrugged. 'I don't know.'

'You're right. You're right. If it was the right decision to keep her here, it would feel better. Her education *is* important but I can't send her away. I need her with me, near me. I will not let her have the same disjointed childhood I was forced to endure.'

'Understood. I do, however, have one other question.'

'Uh-huh? What's that?'

'Why do *you* need to stay here in Tarparnii?'

He gave her a blank look. 'I work here.'

'I know. Why do you need to stay, though?'

'Because this is my home.' He spread his arms wide. 'PMA needs good doctors. They've agreed to support Tarparnii, to send medical personal and supplies, and all of it is vital to my country.'

'Agreed, but you haven't answered the question. Why do *you* need to be here? People have changed jobs in the past.'

'Are you saying I should leave PMA? Leave Tarparnii?' His tone was getting angry now and she hadn't meant to upset him.

Melora shrugged. 'I'm not trying to tell you what

to do, Daniel. I'm merely asking why you're limiting yourself. Why can't Simone receive a good education in another country *with you there*?'

'You mean, move back to England? Take Simone to England with me? Leave Tarparnii?'

'I don't think you could ever really *leave* Tarparnii, Daniel. It's such an intrinsic part of you, but it was just a thought.' She shrugged. 'Over the years I devoted so much of my life to my career. Working hard, securing the right placements, writing articles, undertaking research, doing what needed to be done in order to gain the job I'd always wanted, and when I finally reached my goals, when I thought I was where I wanted to be—great prospects, marriage on the horizon, time to start a family—it was all taken away with one simple lump I found in my breast.

'In a matter of weeks my entire world came crumbling down. I had scans, tests, appointments, concern, worry, decisions. My operating lists were handed on to another surgeon, my clinic lists divided up among my colleagues, my research finished off by my assistant, my engagement broken. For the first time in my life I wasn't in control. I wasn't the one driving my life forward, the cancer was.

'Coming here, to this incredible country, meeting the most accepting and loving people I've ever met in my entire life…it's changed me. It's helped me. You said on my very first day here that you hoped I would find healing here and I have.'

'I'm glad.' His words were deep, personal and full of true meaning.

'But the point I'm trying to make is that I discovered the hard way that work is not the be-all and end-all of my existence. Neither should it be for you. Simone is much more important than your job with PMA.'

'I've been spending more time with her. I've been focusing on her and—'

'And has it worked? Daniel, you need balance in your life. Everyone does. We need to make room for work and play and family and friends and happiness…and love.' Her voice broke on the last word because she knew within that very moment, and with perfect clarity, that she loved him. She loved him and his daughter.

She watched him, standing there, his hands in his pockets as though to keep himself from touching her, and her heart pounded with love for him. She knew he had other concerns, namely Simone, to deal with, and she would never dream of asking him to forgo that, but being here with him, being close to him day in, day out, would become increasingly difficult.

'I'd compartmentalised my life so neatly that before coming here I hadn't realised that one part of my life links with the others. If it doesn't, I end up in a big old mess rather than becoming whole.' She pulled the cardigan closer around her. Watching him, wanting him, loving him and not being able to have him would be the next challenge she would face.

'Don't look at me like that, Mel.'

'Like what, Daniel?'

'Like you want me to hold you, to kiss you.'

'I do,' she whispered. 'I *really* do…but I understand why you can't and I respect that, but it doesn't stop me from wanting it.'

'I know.' His hands came out of his pockets and just for an instant she thought he was going to cross to her side and haul her close, pressing her body to his as they gave in to the yearning and need and desperation that seemed to be surrounding them… but he quickly crossed his arms over his chest and took a small step away. Decision reached.

The sun's rays were starting to peek through the clouds and the humidity of the day was starting to increase. The birds were starting to sing and within another few minutes Simone would wake up. Daniel would become engrossed in his daughter and his work once more and Melora would work hard to keep her distance and deal with this latest twist in her life.

She was in love with a man who couldn't love her back.

Later that morning everyone assisted in packing the transport trucks. Sue, Keith and Melora said their goodbyes to all their friends.

'Thank you so much for having me to stay,' Melora said as she hugged Meeree.

'You have learned much, Melora Washington, and we will see you soon.'

'But I won't be coming back here. We're leaving from the other village to go straight to the airport.'

Meeree's smile was indulgent. 'That is not what I meant. Your heart has been changed.' She touched a hand to Melora's cheek. 'Until we next meet, *Separ.*'

Melora had been shocked to realise that Meeree could see that she was in love with Daniel. Could everyone? Was it that obvious? Before she could ask any more questions, Simone came bounding over.

'I'm so excited, Melora. I get to go with you and I get to see Nahkala. I'm getting on the truck now. Come on.' She took Melora's hand in hers and tugged her along.

'Nahkala, the mother of Daniel, will be as happy to welcome you to her village as I was here. Go. Enjoy. Be safe,' Meeree called, and Melora allowed herself to be led away.

As the trucks rumbled along, Melora pulled out her small sketch pad and a pencil and began to doodle.

'What are you drawing?' a little voice asked, and Melora looked up to see Simone watching her closely. The child was sitting next to her father on the opposite side of the large transport truck.

'Just some of the trees you have here. We don't have them back in Australia.'

'Really? That's funny. Do you have that tree?' Simone pointed to one far in the distance as they drove by.

'No.'

'What about the red bushes?'

'Red bushes?' Melora asked.

'She means the *kapordhe* bushes. I believe you

were sketching them yesterday, around the back of the clinic building,' Daniel offered as he placed a protective arm about his daughter, keeping her close to him as the truck bumped up and down.

She was surprised that he'd seen her. As far as she'd known, he'd been giving her a wide berth. Since their talk that morning he'd again withdrawn into his shell, keeping busy, organising everything for the next few days. Now, sitting on the truck, there was a slight tension between them but both were determined to ignore it—if only for Simone's sake. 'Oh. No. We don't have them in Australia.'

'Well, what do you have?' Simone asked.

'We have gum trees and we have bottle-brush trees and flowers with funny names like kangaroo paw.'

Simone giggled. 'That is funny. I thought a kangaroo was a hoppy animal.'

'It is. Here.' Melora turned a page in her sketch pad and quickly sketched a picture of a kangaroo and then a kangaroo paw flower. Simone was impressed.

'Can you draw me?' she asked.

'I'm not very good with portraits but I can try. You'll need to sit as still as possible, which might be a bit difficult at the moment.'

'And draw Daddy, too,' Simone instructed.

Melora met Daniel's gaze to see if he objected but he merely shrugged one shoulder so she began to draw. It felt strange being able to have an excuse to stare at Daniel, especially when she was usually trying to sneak glances. Now, though, she had the opportunity to capture him, to absorb the angular lines that made his face perfect, his nose, his stubble-covered jaw, his incredibly expressive eyes.

When she had finished, she held out the sketch pad so they could view her handiwork.

'Not good at drawing portraits,' Daniel scoffed ironically, clearly impressed with what he saw. 'You understated your talent, Melora. That looks just like us, doesn't it, Simone?'

The little girl was stunned as she looked at the picture of herself. 'Wow!' The word was breathed with awe and Melora felt a warm and fuzzy glow spread through her at the combination of father and daughter showing her their appreciation. Daniel looked over at her above Simone's head. The child was still exclaiming about the drawing. There, in his rich brown gaze, she saw a gentle caress, as though he was not only appreciating her talent but also thanking her for making his daughter happy.

When she smiled back at him, the look turned from one of thanks to one of need and Melora felt as though a burning hot sensation of desire had shot from him, penetrating the defences she was still scrambling to erect. How could he make her entire body tremble, make her breathing escalate and her heart pound wildly with just one look?

She was unable to look away, even though he was creating havoc with her equilibrium.

'Daniel…' she began when the loud screeching of truck brakes pierced the air. The PMA transport truck was braking rapidly, the action jolting them all around and onto each other. Daniel automatically reached out for Melora while his other arm stayed firmly around Simone's waist. Eventually, when they came to a stop, for a split second no one moved.

'What was that?' The question was out of her mouth before she could stop it. Obviously something was wrong or they wouldn't have stopped.

'I don't know. I'll need to check it out.' He looked down at Simone then back at Melora. He had no idea what danger might be around them and how he was going to protect them from it. Simone was his baby girl, his world, and he'd vowed to B'lana that he would take care of her. Melora, however, was the woman he simply could not stop thinking about. The fact that she'd become so very important to him in such a very short time was undeniable, and he wanted to keep her safe as well.

Melora and Simone. He had to protect them.

'Are you hurt, *Separ*?' he asked his daughter, his hands quickly running over her to make sure she didn't have any bumps or bruises and that her cast was still intact.

'I'm fine, Daddy.'

'Good. Melora?'

'I'm fine.'

Daniel looked around at the rest of his crew. 'Everyone OK?'

'Yes,' they all replied.

'We go and look,' Belhara said to Daniel, who nodded in agreement.

'Melora, would you mind holding Simone?'

'Sure.' Melora quickly held out her arms and Simone needed no more coaxing than that, leaving her father's arms to go to the safety of Melora's. He stood and started making his way through the truck, and just before he was about to jump off the end, Melora couldn't help but call, 'Be careful.'

Goodness only knew what they would find. Would it be soldiers? Soldiers with guns? Friend or foe?

Daniel's answer was to look at her over his shoulder, grin and wink, sending a rioting shock wave of goose-bumps through her.

'Always.'

CHAPTER TEN

'It's an emergency,' Daniel said, appearing at the rear of the truck a minute later. 'Simone, come and sit up front in the truck with Perry, the driver. You remember Perry,' he said as he lifted her from the truck and carried her round to the driver's door.

'Hi, Perry,' Simone said cheerfully. 'Look at my arm.'

'How on earth did you do that?' Perry asked, and Simone started to tell him the whole story.

'That should keep her busy,' Melora remarked from behind Daniel, and it was only then he realised that she'd climbed out of the truck. 'What's the situation?' she asked as they headed back to the rear of the truck to collect supplies.

'An old car has crashed. Wrapped around the tree.'

'How many people on board?' Sue asked as she quickly pulled a few of the portable medi-kits from the containers they'd packed in the rear of the truck.

'I did a brief head count. Made at least five. Could be more. Perry's calling it in.'

'At *least* five?' Melora's eyebrows hit her hairline. 'But doesn't the car only seat four?'

'Not many people have transport,' Daniel replied. 'So if a car is headed in a specific direction, people just hop on board. Everybody ready?' he asked as the team assembled. 'Good. Let's go.' Daniel quickly blew a kiss to Simone before leading his team forward.

By now, as they'd been working together for some time, they all shifted into their specific areas. Bel and P'Ko-lat did a sort of triage, Richard called for Keith to come and take a look at a patient who had multiple fractures, Belhara was working with Sue to help stabilise and talk to one of the young teenagers who had been thrown clear of the wreckage to find out exactly what had happened.

Daniel had walked over to the wreckage, calling for Melora to grab a medi-kit and follow him. She gasped when she saw the vehicle. It wasn't a sturdy Jeep like the one she'd travelled in with Daniel but a small old car, circa 1950s, which appeared to be held together by string and tape, the rust doing its best to break it all apart. The roof of the car had been cut away a long time ago, no doubt in order to hold more people. The large, firm tree trunk, however, had penetrated the bonnet, smashing through the engine and ending up almost in the driver's seat.

'Most of the hangers-on would have been knocked clear when the vehicle hit the tree but not these guys.' Daniel's words were direct but filled with compassion as they carefully went closer to see to the people most affected by the crash. The smell of petrol was in the air and both of them recognised this fact.

It was clear that the driver was dead, impaled through the heart by a large branch, but Daniel still pressed his fingers to the man's carotid pulse to confirm it. There were two people and a lot of baggage, items wrapped in large blankets all crammed into the back seat, and one person in the front passenger seat. Melora went round to the passenger side, stepping carefully through the debris of bits of car panelling, leaves, twigs and other things in order to get to where she needed to be. All the time she was mentally going through what she needed to do.

She was finding it difficult to come to terms with the fact that this MVA was just like the ones she'd assisted with back in Australia. For some silly reason she'd thought that out here in the jungle she wouldn't see this sort of accident. There were no six-lane highways here, no freeways, no cement flyovers, and yet here she was, assisting at an MVA that was just as intense as the ones she'd attended back home.

While she wanted to look and watch and understand how this could have happened, to grasp the fact that there had been so many people in such a small vehicle, to compare this country with her own, she had a job to do. Nothing mattered except doing what she did best.

She put the medi-kit on the ground at her feet and pressed her fingers to the neck of the woman in the front passenger seat. 'Pulse is weak.' She called to the woman but received no answer. She shifted to help Daniel check the people in the back. 'This young man is dead,' she reported of the teenager closest to her, noting how even if he'd somehow managed to survive the enormous visible damage to his skull, he would have suffered from massive brain damage.

'The girl has a pulse but still not as strong as I'd hoped,' Daniel told her after checking the other passenger in the back. 'These blankets crammed around her no doubt cushioned her from much of the impact.' He shook his head at the image before him. It wasn't the first time he'd come across such an accident and this one was nowhere near as bad as others as it appeared there had been a total of about eight or nine people involved. Sometimes the roads out here, especially after rains, could be as treacherous as any of the roads back in England.

'Right,' he said to Melora. 'Let's get them out so we can treat them.'

'We just shift them out?'

'There's no time for stabilising before moving. This car is volatile and even if we cause more injuries along the way, it's better than getting blown up.'

'Blown up!' This country was so different from her own. Coming here, she'd expected to be treating gunshot wounds, or giving immunisations, or doing minor surgical operations, and even then she'd had her eyes opened, especially after performing emergency surgery on Meimii, but attending an accident where the car might blow up?

Again, she realised there was no fire brigade coming to douse the area with foam to protect against such an event. There were no ambulances on their way to help out with the casualties. *They* were the help and if she didn't get her thought processes back in focus, she wouldn't be able to provide much of that.

Daniel came around to her side and together they managed to shift the woman in the front passenger seat, carrying her to a safer area. Melora collected her medi-kit and checked the woman while Daniel called for Richard and Belhara to help him pull out the front seat of the car to give them better access to the people in the back.

'The petrol leak is not too large,' Melora heard Belhara remark, and within another moment she was joined by Sue, who helped her to stabilise the patient as best they could.

'What will happen to all these people? The ones who are still alive?' Melora asked. 'They need more treatment, they need more care. We don't have any facilities out here, only the medical supplies we've brought with us. What do we do?'

Daniel could hear the heartbreak in Melora's voice as he and Belhara carried over the young girl from the back seat. They placed her on the ground near where Melora knelt.

'I've had our driver radio for another transport. We'll shift as many as we can to my mother's village. They have a clinic building there with supplies. Apart from that...' he met her gaze and she could see the pain and suffering he felt '...we do whatever we can.'

And that was the entire reason why she'd come here, not only to find some peace within her own life but to give to others. In looking outwards, she'd been able to heal inwards, and as her gaze held Daniel's for a split second, she could see that he was as much affected by what was happening around them as she was. This great man loved his country, loved giving help and support on a daily basis. He was truly amazing.

'OK.' Melora nodded and returned her thoughts back to her patients. As the older woman was as stable as possible, she shifted to work on the young girl, running her hands over limbs and bones and feeling her way to some sort of diagnosis. She used her penlight torch to check the girl's eyes and then hooked a stethoscope into her ears, listening to the heart, the lungs and the abdomen.

'Pupils equal and reacting to light, fracture to right arm as there is no radial pulse on that side, distended abdomen, possible bladder rupture due to patient voiding, and head injury. High probability of internal bleeding.'

Keith came over and rechecked the girl's bones. 'Fractured pelvis, or so it feels.'

'That could account for the internal inju—'

'Melora!' Daniel's tone was insistent and she immediately stood and headed over to where he was. He was kneeling on the ground next to a child of about eight who had been thrown from the car. The child had a large slash across the abdomen as well as having an arm and leg twisted at odd angles.

'I thought it seemed odd that the woman in the front seat was all alone. She had no paraphernalia around her, which meant she'd no doubt been holding someone. The orthopaedic fractures are clean breaks but…' he pointed to the child's red-stained abdomen '…take a look.'

Melora pulled on a fresh pair of gloves and felt gingerly around. 'I need light. Have we got a torch?'

Daniel pulled one from his pocket and shined it in the area.

'Right, I'll need gauze, packing, a clamp and double-zero Vicryl. As the child is still unconscious, let's get to work.'

Daniel arranged for one of the less injured passengers to come and hold the torch while he pulled on some gloves to assist Melora in this impromptu surgery. She debrided the wound as best she could before finding the offending arteries and suturing them closed.

Bel had come over and inserted a saline drip, which would help replace fluids. Melora was almost finished when the child started to regain consciousness but Belhara was on hand to administer a sedative in order to keep the child still while Melora finished what she was doing.

After suturing the wound closed, Bel applied a sterile bandage while Daniel took a look at the boy's arm, carefully manipulating the bones back into a more stable alignment before splinting them into place.

'His blood pressure is more improved,' Bel announced, and Melora gave a little sigh of satisfaction.

Daniel was kneeling beside her, finishing off his bandaging, and looked at her with a mixture of pride and happiness. She was such a remarkable woman. Life here in Tarparnii was very different from her own world in Australia, and yet whenever a different situation was presented to her, she took a moment to readjust and then dived right in. 'Good work,' he said softly.

She swallowed. 'Thanks.' The word was but a whisper. They looked into each other's eyes for a moment longer before both of them jolted back into their professional personas. 'What's the status on the other patients?' she asked, rising to her feet and pulling off her gloves. She headed in one direction, Daniel headed in the other, but even as they worked, continuing to provide medical care to the people who needed it, she was acutely aware of his whereabouts at any given moment.

When the second transport truck arrived, bringing extra bamboo stretchers and supplies, they were able to load the most critical patients into that truck. The people who had either jumped or been thrown clear of the impact and had, therefore, only suffered less extensive injuries boarded the medical transport along with Simone, Sue and Bel.

As they were packing up, some of the soldiers arrived at the scene and Melora recognised one of them as Daniel's cousin, Paul. The two men spoke gravely for about five minutes, Daniel explaining as much as he knew. They walked to the front of the vehicle and were looking at it when Melora climbed into the truck to monitor the more critical patients.

Out of the four people they'd found in the car, only two had survived and neither of them had regained consciousness as yet. The total number of people involved in the accident had been nine and as Melora checked on the eight-year-old boy, pleased he seemed to be doing much better, she knew there was still much to be done.

Daniel climbed into the truck just as she'd finished doing observations on the two unconscious women from the car. Keith was monitoring the two other critical patients and Belhara was keeping a close eye on the boy.

'Reports?' he asked as the truck rumbled to life, taking them to their destination. They all filled him in on the status of the patients and by the time they arrived in the village where Daniel's mother lived, Melora was positive the young girl with the pelvic fracture would require immediate surgery to stabilise her.

Their arrival at the village of his mother was not what Daniel had initially planned, the trucks basically pulling up and carting their patients directly to the clinic, where another three PMA staff were in residence. Melora and Keith along with Belhara as anaesthetist went directly into the 'operating room' with the young girl.

It was three hours later that they finally came out, Melora looking weary and ready for a sleep.

'How is she?' Daniel could see how exhausted Melora was and wanted to haul her into his arms, hold her close, support her weight, tell her to rest her head. He wanted to take her tension and make it disappear like a magic trick. He wanted to massage her shoulders to relieve her anxiety and when he realised his palms were itching to touch her, to help her, he quickly clasped them together.

'She's stable. Any other news on the rest of the patients?' She closed her eyes, listening to his report, and was pleased to hear that the other woman from the car had regained consciousness and was improving.

'They are mother and daughter. The driver was her *par'machkai* and the other teenage boy in the car was her son. At least we have managed to save two of her children.'

'Oh, the poor woman. To lose so much!'

Daniel heard the crack in her voice, her words so heartfelt and filled with compassion. She cared. Melora *really* cared about these people and he couldn't take it any longer. Without a word he stepped forward, placing his arms about her, urging her closer, and by some miracle, instead of pushing him away, especially after he'd already told her he needed to focus his attention on Simone, she drew close to him…needing him as much as he needed her.

Her arms came instantly around him, both of them offering and receiving comfort in the wake of the devastation they'd witnessed. Such loss, such heartache, such pain.

'Along with Keith, you have saved her daughter. That will mean a lot.' He spoke softly near her ear, breathing in the intoxicating scent of the woman he found difficult to resist.

'I hate MVAs,' she murmured against his chest, breathing him in, desperate to make a memory, to recall every tiny detail about this man who she knew she could never be with. Worlds apart. 'I guess I hadn't thought I'd come across them here.'

'Sort of jolts you back into reality. One minute you're sketching and the next you're suturing.' And it *had* jolted him back to reality because even though he knew on a logical level that there really couldn't be any future for himself and Melora together, he was desperate to keep her safe, to protect her, to be near her—for ever.

He'd tried to deny such feelings, he'd tried to push them to the rear of his mind and to focus on keeping his daughter safe, doing his job, doing what was expected of him, but surely he could find some room in his life to keep this woman close?

Melora eased back, knowing if she didn't make some sort of move to put distance between them she might just want to stay in the secure embrace of his arms for the rest of her life. She looked up at him and noticed that although his brows were drawn together in confusion, there was also repressed desire in his eyes.

'When I'm in your arms,' she whispered, 'I feel as though I can cope with such situations as we've just come through. You give me...' But she shouldn't. She couldn't tell Daniel that he gave her strength, that ever since he'd come into her life her world had become enriched. Where there had been pain, he'd brought healing. Where there had been lack of self-confidence, he'd boosted her up. Where there had been hopelessness, he'd shown her how to hope.

She didn't want to put any extra pressure on him, let him know that she'd come to rely on him. He had big decisions to face because if he *did* decide to take Simone out of the country in the pursuit of her education, it would mean that *he* would have to leave Tarparnii. His work, his friends, his family...his life. There was no place for her in such a decision. This was something he needed to figure out and although she wanted nothing more than to suggest he come and live in Australia for a while, to investigate the schooling system in a country that was much closer to Tarparnii than England, and that he think about *his* needs as well as those of his daughter, she didn't feel she had the right to put so much pressure on him.

As she continued to look into his eyes, her own heart radiating love for him, Melora knew she was moving deeper and deeper into the fire, wanting to be with him, to be close to him, wanting to have what she couldn't have.

She didn't care where they were, who was around them or what else was happening in the world. Right now, at this point in her life, she was accepting the fact that being in Daniel's arms, feeling that same surge of longing and need pass through both of them, only succeeded in enhancing the intense emotions she already felt for him.

'I give you…what?' he prompted quietly.

She paused before answering, breathing in and out, allowing his scent to wash over her, to relax her. 'You give me strength, Daniel.' The words were barely a whisper. 'And I thank you for that.'

'Oh, Melora.' He exhaled and tightened his hold

on her as though he never wanted to let her go. 'You are important to me. Please don't think you're not. But—'

'I know. I know,' she interjected. 'We come from different worlds. We have different circumstances to face. Me with reconstructive surgery, and you with Simone's education.'

'Our lives are on separate paths,' he confirmed. 'And I wish that it could be different. I wish we'd met each other at a different point in our lives, when these issues weren't so relevant.'

'It just wasn't meant to be.'

There was such sadness in her eyes, such desolation and despair in her voice, and Daniel's heart turned over with yearning. He wanted this woman. He was through denying it and even though he knew he shouldn't, he urged her closer, tightening his arms around her, the need to kiss her, even if it was just once, was something he desperately desired. It wasn't often he gave in to his own desires but right here, right now, in this one brief moment, he needed to.

Neither of them spoke, both of them caught up in the sensations that surrounded them. She was only there for a few more days. After that she would be gone from his life for ever. He wanted to hold her, to touch her, to kiss her, and this might be his one and only opportunity to do that.

He knew it was wrong. He knew he shouldn't allow them to traverse this path, knowing that it could lead to even stronger heartache, but the longing, the need, the overwhelming desire to press his lips to hers were becoming too hard to fight.

'Mel…' She was looking at his mouth, watching the way his lips formed her name. When her tongue came out to lick the plump, pink lips, as though she was just waiting for him and him alone, something deep within him snapped and he edged closer.

He had never felt this strongly about any woman since B'lana and that in itself spoke volumes. Melora was intelligent, she was honest and she was absolutely divine. She loved Simone, he could see it whenever the two of them were together. The 'bright' girls, their hair shining in the sunlight. Melora was important to him and the sensations whirring around them, their pheromones, mixing and combining together, were becoming too intoxicating to ignore.

'Daniel,' she whispered, the distance between their mouths now barely millimetres. 'Please?' There was a slight pleading, a slight question and a lot of need radiating from her. She wanted this. He wanted this.

With their hearts beating wildly in unison, the rest of the world disappearing from around them, their mouths finally came into contact with each other.

Melora sighed into the kiss, unable to believe that Daniel was actually kissing her but at the same time enjoying every passing second. His mouth was soft and sensual, not hot and demanding, as she'd thought it might have been. He wasn't pressuring her, he wasn't forcing her into anything she didn't want and instead was taking his time, as though he was savouring every new sensation.

Cherished.

That was the way his touch, his hold made her feel. It was as though now that they were here, he wanted to take his time, to make it last and to burn it into his memory. His hand at her back was warm and firm, his thumb moving in little circles, each tiny motion causing a new flood of tingling awareness to course through her.

Never had any man kissed her in such a way. He not only made her feel safe and secure but he made her feel cherished and treasured. She was important...to him. And when he opened his mouth a little wider, his tongue gently caressing her lower lip, she gave up any remnants of control. She wanted to get lost in the passion and the pleasure that was Daniel Tarvon.

As though by mutual consent, they deepened the kiss, the flavours of her mouth, the sweetness of her scent, the delight of her body so close to his a memory he would hold close for ever. This woman, this most special, most precious woman who had been through so much, who was far stronger than she realised, was building a response in him he'd never felt before.

The fact that he wanted to hold her close and protect her for as long as he possibly could was something he could rationalise and come to terms with, but the way she was setting his body alight, with the way her response to him was firing up a furnace that he doubted would ever burn out, was something he hadn't expected at all.

The woman was intoxicating. Melora Washington's luscious lips, opened to his own, accepting his touch, her body as close to his as she dared get, was enough to show him how incredible she was. The scent of freshness, the scent he equated with her was mingling with his own scent and the pheromones they were creating between them became a heady concoction, driving them both forward.

He'd wanted this moment—the one he now realised had been inevitable from about five seconds after he'd been made aware of her presence at the airport—to last far longer than he knew it could, but oxygen, or the lack there of, was starting to become a necessary factor for him to consider… soon.

When she sighed and leaned into him, he brought her nearer, the need to have her as close as possible becoming almost too much to bear.

The sound of someone else clearing their throat behind them made Melora freeze, her eyes snapping opening to look intently into his.

'Daniel?' The female voice was accented but rich and mature in its tones.

Daniel slowly relaxed his hold on Melora but didn't let her go even as she swivelled in his arms.

'Melora.' His voice was deep, personal and very close to her ear, as he held out a hand to the woman before them. 'May I introduce you to Nahkala. My mother.'

CHAPTER ELEVEN

His *mother*!

Melora was quick to disengage herself from Daniel and, trying not to blush at having been caught in such a compromising position by his *mother*, she stepped forward and took the woman's outstretched hands, pleased she knew enough Tarparnese now to greet his mother properly.

'You are very welcome,' Nahkala said in her perfectly modulated English. 'I am sorry that your arrival in my village was not all it should have been but we all appreciate your gifts in saving the lives of our people.'

'Thank you. I am honoured to be here and to be so warmly welcomed by you,' Melora replied, and then was surprised when Nahkala let go of her hands, only to place a warm hand against her cheek.

'How could I not welcome the woman who has rescued my Daniel?' After a brief moment Nahkala stepped back. 'Please, excuse me. I can hear my grandchild calling my name. I do miss her.'

Melora watched Daniel's mother go, admiring the way she seemed to glide with authority and grace. She turned to face Daniel. 'Rescued?'

Daniel shook his head. 'Sometimes she mixes up the translation of English words. Don't worry about it. Right now we need to check on the rest of our patients and then have something to eat.'

Melora was too tired to argue and allowed him to lead the way. She still couldn't believe that he'd kissed her, that it had been completely amazing and that all she wanted was more, more, more. Pleasure was mixed with pain as she worked hard to put mental distance between them. They both knew that this attraction, which only seemed to grow more intense every moment they spent together, couldn't lead anywhere permanent.

They'd only be fooling themselves if they thought otherwise and Melora prided herself on not being a fool. Focusing on work, on the people around them, seemed to be the order for the rest of the day. Nahkala and the people of her village were holding their own version of a welcoming banquet for all the new and familiar people who had come to help out.

The banquet involved some of the younger women doing a native dance and some of the young men showing off their hunting skills as they pretended to hunt the shadows cast by the fire. Melora enjoyed it all immensely but as the evening progressed, she made sure there was distance between herself and Daniel.

He'd kissed her. It had been one of the most incredible events in her life. It had shown her that even though she may consider her body unattractive and maybe even deformed, Daniel most certainly didn't see her that way at all. When he'd held her, he'd made her feel soft and gentle and pretty and highly feminine.

It went a long way to boosting her self-confidence, which had been seriously damaged. Now, though, if she looked at herself through his eyes, she saw a woman who was a survivor. Not only had she survived breast cancer and the incapacitating treatments that went along with it, but that she'd survived Leighton's dismissal of her. Through Daniel's eyes, she saw herself as strong, desirable, a woman of substance…a woman who was more than capable of facing her uncertain future.

After the celebrations and before she turned in for the night, she checked on their patients once more, talking to Bel and Keith, who were doing the first night shift. When she was satisfied with the statuses, she headed to the hut where she'd been told she was sleeping. Richard, Sue and Belhara were already lying down on their mats, half-asleep as they chatted to the three other staff members who resided permanently in this village.

'Where's Daniel?' she asked as she unpacked her bag, hoping the question came out sounding nonchalant, even though she felt as though she was drawing attention to herself simply by asking.

'He's sleeping in his mother's hut,' Sue told her. 'Apparently, Simone fell asleep on Nahkala's shoulder at the end of the celebrations. The little darling looked so gorgeous.' Sue yawned as she'd finished speaking.

Melora nodded, feeling lost and sad and bereft at the fact that she hadn't been able to say goodnight to Simone. Her throat started to ache and her eyes started to itch as she worked valiantly to hold back tears.

She knew she had no cause to complain. Nahkala was Simone's grandmother and of course she and Daniel would be staying in his mother's hut, rather than bunking down with the rest of the PMA crew. It was silly to feel so upset about that, about feeling as though she'd been shut out once again from Daniel's life.

He'd kissed her.

She had known at the time that it couldn't change anything, had warred with herself about going through with it, but, of course, she'd been unable to resist him, especially when he had been the one to reach for her as she'd exited the hospital. He'd been the one to touch her, comfort her, hold her close.

He'd kissed her…and nothing had changed. He still had his life. She still had hers. The world would keep turning and time would continue to pass. Simone would be cared for by those around her and Daniel would come to an arrangement about the importance of her education. She would return to Australia, focus on her reconstructive surgery and then decide what to do with the rest of her life.

Coming here to Tarparnii had shown her that there was much more to life than what she'd settled for over the years. She'd always thought that having had cancer was a bad thing, but surviving cancer had forced her to look outside her normal bonds, to see the world through different eyes and to realise there was more to her life than the inside of a hospital.

Loving Daniel, though, had certainly put a spanner in the works. She hadn't expected that to happen at all but accepting it was part of the new process she was learning to follow. The people of Tarparnii had a way of accepting things beyond their control. They would contemplate, absorb and then move on with their lives.

Melora thought about Daniel, sleeping in his mother's hut beside his daughter, who would no doubt be quietly slumbering, her head resting on her frilly, pink, pillow as she nuzzled close to her father. Simone was as much a part of her as Daniel was, and as she lay there and closed her eyes, she knew that she would not trade her time here in Tarparnii for anything in the world. Never had she thought she would feel as though her life was back on track and never had she thought she'd be able to open her heart and love another.

She only hoped that when she left, returning to her world in Australia, her heart would be able to continue to move forward, that her love for Daniel would diminish over time and that she would be able to think of her wonderful time here in Tarparnii without the pang of regret that pierced her heart even now. Silently, though, she doubted she would ever stop loving him or his gorgeous daughter.

'I wish we'd met each other at a different point in our lives.'

Daniel's words ran around her head and as she closed her eyes tighter, clutching her hands to her chest, she wished it could be that way, too.

'Goodnight, my loves,' she whispered quietly into the dark.

Over the next days they ran several clinics, which usually started before the sun came up and ended long after it had set. Simone was as bubbly and as bright as usual, getting nearly everyone she met to sign her cast.

'There's no more room left,' she told Melora one day, showing off her cast. The little girl was still very generous with her cuddles and kisses and had insisted on having Melora read the bedtime story every night.

Nahkala was a quietly spoken woman who tended to observe more than she talked.

'When you stop and you listen to people,' Nahkala said, the night before Melora was due to leave Tarparnii, 'that is when their hearts tell you what they are really feeling.'

Melora had just finished reading Simone a bedtime story, and the two women were sitting and watching the child sleep. 'That's how I feel with Simone. I love spending time with her. She is a wonderful girl. Daniel has done an amazing job so far and will no doubt continue to do so.'

'You hold my son in high esteem.' Nahkala's words were a statement and Melora knew there was no getting around it. Honesty was valued with these people and she respected that.

'Yes. Very.'

'Your heart, when you look at him, is filled with love.'

Melora looked over at Simone, then back at Nahkala. 'Yes.'

'It is right,' Nahkala said with a bright smile. 'You are a woman of great integrity, *Separ*. I am thankful that my son has chosen well.'

'Oh, no.' Melora quickly shook her head, instantly pushing back the tears that sprang to her eyes. 'Daniel and I are not together. I'm leaving to return to Australia tomorrow and Daniel has some big decisions to make. There is very little chance we'll see each other again.'

Nahkala reached over and took one of Melora's hands in hers. 'There are many paths that love can take, Melora. Some are straight, some are winding, some are of great surprise, and some have mountains that need to be patiently traversed.'

Melora smiled. 'I think Daniel and I must have the last three combined.'

'What seems impossible is not. The two of you still have some work to accomplish.' She brushed her free hand down Melora's cheek with motherly concern. It was touching. 'You must have the faith, *Separ.*'

Melora nodded and looked over at Simone, swallowing and trying to get her emotions back under control. 'Faith?'

'Faith in yourself and in Daniel.' After a short pause Nahkala let Melora go before rising gracefully to her feet. 'It is time for you to rest. Tomorrow will be eventful.'

'Yes.' Melora leaned over Simone and pressed one last kiss to the sleeping child's forehead before standing. 'Thank you, Nahkala.'

'You are most welcome, *Separ.*'

As Melora left Nahkala's hut, she headed across the now deserted village clearing just as Daniel was coming out of the clinic. Her heart leapt with delight when she saw him but it was swiftly followed by a deep and powerful ache. Within a matter of hours she would be leaving him.

Ever since their kiss the other day, both of them had worked hard at maintaining a professional distance, knowing that any acceleration of what they might be feeling towards each other couldn't be. She had her life in Australia and he had his life here with Simone. To deepen the feelings they had for each other, to give in and touch and kiss and simply enjoy spending whatever free time they had together, would have only made their inevitable parting that much worse.

Daniel stopped walking the instant he saw her but after a moment shoved his hands into his pockets and came in her direction. 'Simone asleep?' he asked.

Melora's smile was always easy when they talked of his daughter. He could see quite clearly just how much she loved Simone and also how much Simone loved Melora. Never before had his daughter bonded so completely with another woman. Never before had Daniel bonded so instantly with a woman as he had with Melora. He dug his hands deeper into his pockets.

'Yes. She's an angel.'

He chuckled. 'When she sleeps? I'd agree with that. A perfect angel.'

'I didn't mean it like that. She's an angel all the time, in my eyes.'

'Yes, but you seem to see the best in people, Melora.' His words had softened and with the way he was looking at her, as though she were the most incredible woman in the world, Melora was having a difficult time coping being so close to him.

'Thank you, Daniel. That's a nice thing to say.'

'It's the truth.'

They were both silent, both intensely aware of the other, but they still kept their distance.

'Everything all right at the clinic?' she asked.

'No complications. Patients all sleeping. Sue and Richard are taking the night shift.'

She nodded, pleased to hear that everyone in the clinic was fine. She'd also planned on heading to the clinic, knowing she wouldn't sleep much at all tonight. Every time she thought about leaving here, about returning to her bleak Daniel-and-Simone-less life back in Australia, her throat would close over with sorrow and her eyes would sting with tears. She'd hoped that keeping busy at the clinic tonight might help keep her thoughts at bay.

'Well...' Daniel sidestepped her. 'I'd better

get some sleep. Big day tomorrow. Pack up here and then two trucks headed in very different directions.'

Was he talking about them?

'Anyway, I hope you get some rest tonight, Mel.'

'Mmm-hmm.' She nodded, wanting to reach for him, her heart begging for him to reach for her, to hold her, to tell her that he loved her, that he never wanted her to leave him. She bit her tongue in order to keep herself somewhat under control. He turned and had taken two steps away from her when she called his name. He stopped and turned eagerly to look at her.

'I've been meaning to ask you…'

'Yes?' His eagerness increased.

'What does *Separ* mean?'

'*Separ.*'

'Yes. I've heard you call Simone that a lot of times. I've always meant to ask you what it means and as I leave here in about seven hours' time, I thought now might be the last chance I get.'

He wished she wouldn't talk about leaving because it only caused his heart to ache. '*Separ* is a precious gemstone. They are very rare in Tarparnii now, the government having mined the land many years ago for these exquisitely beautiful stones. They are red and green, blue and purple, pink and orange, with flecks of silver and gold.' He frowned for a moment. 'They are difficult to describe but they are more beautiful than any opal, they are brighter than any diamond. The only time I saw a stone was when I was about eight years old and even then I remember being captivated by the colours when holding it to the light. It was a defining day for me. It was the day when I felt an emotional connection to beauty, when I appreciated it.' He paused then asked, 'Why do you ask now?'

Melora shrugged. 'Your mother...called me *Separ* tonight.'

Daniel processed this information then stepped forward, crossing the distance between them. He knew if he pulled her into his arms he would never let her go and let her go he must so instead he took both of her hands in his and held them tightly.

'She is right to call you that, Melora. You are radiant, you are stunning, and you are incredibly open and honest and beautiful.' Daniel couldn't believe how his voice cracked at the last few words. 'You are a precious gemstone, priceless and greatly appreciated.' And loved.

He swallowed over the dryness in his throat as the words penetrated his mind. He loved Melora? No. He couldn't possibly have fallen in love with her...could he?

Melora put her key into the lock and opened the door to her Sydney apartment, pushing it wearily as her carry bag fell from her shoulder, jolting her elbow. The instant she was inside, she left the bag on the floor by the door, tossed her keys onto the side table and shuffled through the place, not even bothering to turn on any lights.

In her bedroom she slumped down across the bed, not even bothering to take off the coat she'd had to put on at Sydney airport due to the coolness of the evening breeze. Closing her eyes, she pulled a pillow close, hugging it to her before letting the pent-up emotions she felt like she'd been holding onto for an eternity to come to the surface.

Everything was wrong.

Her world was wrong. The plane she'd disembarked from had been large and impersonal. There had been no one waiting for her and she'd come home to a dark and depressing apartment. Even the bed felt far too soft after two weeks of sleeping on a mat on the ground.

She missed the bright cheerful faces of the people from the villages, she missed the native Tarparniian birds singing their songs to wake her in the morning, she missed the thatched, peaked roofline of the huts, she missed...everything.

And everyone.

She missed Simone.

But most of all she missed Daniel.

Daniel. The man she'd fallen in love with.

She had never expected to meet a man who was so incredibly wonderful, who made her feel special and loved and cherished. A man who was such an amazing father to his little girl, determined to do everything he could to give her the best possible upbringing. A man who gave to other people like the heavens gave sunshine and rain. A man who, when he held her close, his lips wreaking havoc with her insides as his mouth moved tenderly over hers, made her feel as though her life had true meaning again.

The phone by her bed started ringing but she ignored it, pulling the pillow tighter, hugging it closer. She didn't want to speak to anyone, didn't want to see anyone, didn't want to do anything. From the moment he'd dropped her hands and walked away from her last night, Melora had felt her heart start to slowly break. When the transport trucks had come to take them to the airport, Daniel had had to forcibly peel a crying Simone from Melora's arms, the child declaring that she wasn't going to let 'her Melora' go.

Daniel had held his sobbing daughter, the tears in his eyes mirroring the devastation in Melora's as he'd stood there and watched as her truck had rumbled away, the distance between them increasing, emulating the pain in her heart.

The two people she loved the most were not with her and that alone was enough to cause her immeasurable pain.

She pulled the other side of the duvet over her, not even bothering to take off her shoes or get changed. Curling into the foetal position, she realised that nothing else mattered in this world. Not her job, not her apartment, not even her impending surgery.

Daniel and Simone.

She'd gone looking for her life and she'd found it, but without Daniel and Simone it was as meaningless as it had been before…perhaps even more so. With tears streaming silently down her face, pains in her chest due to the heart that really did feel as though it was breaking, Melora allowed herself to wallow in sorrow.

'Right, that's it. I'm officially worried about you.' Emmy sat down opposite Melora at her dining-room table. 'You've been back in Australia for three days and you've hardly said a word about Tarparnii other than it was "good". What is that supposed to mean?' Emerson Freeman pushed her long auburn hair back from her shoulders, picked up her coffee cup and glared at her friend.

'It means it was just what I needed. Sort of.'

'Why didn't you call us to come and pick you up from the airport? You've been hibernating here in your apartment ever since you got back, except for seeing your surgeon, and you're not answering any of your calls.' Emmy put her cup down, coffee forgotten, and looked at her friend with concern. 'What happened, Mel?' she asked softly, and it was that soft, caring tone that was Melora's undoing.

As she looked at her friend, she felt her eyes blur with tears and her bottom lip start to quiver. 'So much,' she whispered, and sniffed. 'I went to Tarparnii to try and figure out what had happened to my life and…I got more than I bargained for.'

She swallowed over the lump in her throat and

stood, heading to the tissue box on the coffee table, only to find the box was empty. She went to the box on the kitchen counter but it was empty as well. She pulled off a piece of kitchen paper towel and blew her nose.

Melora leaned against the kitchen bench for a moment, trying to gather her strength to talk to her friend so that Emmy wouldn't continue to be worried about her. After a few deep breaths she headed back to the dining room and sat down, feeling more composed.

'Tell me about your time. What you did? Which villages you stayed at? Did you like the clinic buildings?'

Melora smiled, her mind instantly jumping to the memory of Daniel stroking the bricks. 'The clinic buildings are brilliant, although I have to say I didn't really appreciate them until we travelled to a different village and I had to perform an appendectomy in a tent.'

Emmy smiled and nodded. 'Good times.'

'I helped deliver a baby not long after I arrived. That was…' she thought back to Daniel, delivering the baby, of J'tana holding her baby for the first time and thanking them both so much for stopping to help her '…miraculous.' She sighed with reflected happiness. 'They called me the "bright" doctor because of my blonde hair.'

'Ah, of course.'

'Simone and I were instant friends, mainly because of our hair.'

'Hair colour is very important to almost five-year-old girls.'

'Yes.' Even saying Simone's name was enough to cause pain in Melora's heart. 'Meeree and Jalak are in excellent health, as always, and Daniel introduced me to his mother, Nahkala.'

'She's an incredible woman, in charge of a very large village and all on her own. That's pioneering stuff in Tarparnii but Nahkala is wise and just. Tarvon definitely takes after her. Caring and protecting people. Just like his mother.'

'Yes. He is good at that.' Melora sipped her coffee, not tasting a thing as she tried to steer her thoughts away from Daniel. She missed him far too much to think about him because when she did, when she allowed herself to contemplate all that she had lost, how her life had changed completely from black to white, her overactive tear ducts started to do their thing again.

'Sue was there.' Melora informed her friend.

'Along with Keith and Richard. They were great and, of course, Bel and Belhara and P'Ko-lat.'

'Sounds as though you were working with a great team.'

'I was.'

'And Tarvon is an excellent leader.'

'The best,' she said with a heartfelt sigh.

'He's quite a guy.'

'You have no idea.' The words were out of her mouth before she could stop them and she quickly put her cup down and closed her eyes.

'Was that a slip of the tongue, my friend? I know something happened in Tarparnii, something big.'

'How can you know that?' she asked, opening her eyes and standing, needing some space.

'You've shut yourself away, Melora.' Emmy spread her arms wide. 'It doesn't take rocket science to figure out that something was wrong. What *really* happened?'

Melora bit her lip then shrugged, deciding she needed someone to talk to.

'I fell in love.' The words came out on rush and the instant they were out she wished them back. Their love could never be. Different worlds. Daniel needed to focus on Simone, to make sure he provided the best education and care for his child, while she had multiple reconstructive surgeries to undergo. Their lives were just too different…but that wouldn't always be the case, a little voice deep inside her heart whispered.

Perhaps once the surgeries were over, after she'd made a complete recovery, she could go back to Tarparnii, or to England, to wherever Daniel and his gorgeous girl were. At that thought a small sliver of hope started to grow. Could it be possible? Did he care for her in that way? Did he love her?

'Love?' Emmy's eyebrows hit her hairline. 'With Tarvon?'

Melora's eyes widened. 'How do you know?'

'I don't know anything. I'm just guessing, but given the fact that he's taken to calling Dart via the satellite phone on a daily basis since you returned to Australia, simply to find out how you are, well, that sort of gave us a clue.' Emmy clasped her hands to her chest. 'You really fell in love with him?'

'Yes. He's been calling?' She couldn't believe it.

'Yes.'

'Why didn't he call me?' Perhaps he simply

wanted to know that she was all right and hadn't really wanted to talk.

'Hmm…let me think…have you been answering your phone since you returned?'

'Oh, no.' Melora closed her eyes and shook her head. How could she have been so stupid? She'd been so wrapped up in her own misery that she hadn't wanted to talk to anyone. Daniel had tried to call her? Could that be true?

'The man's been beside himself with worry for you and when neither Dart nor I could get hold of you, it was time to take action.'

'I'm sorry.'

'You should be. We were all worried. Poor Tarvon has been crazy with concern.'

There was a knock at her front door and Melora frowned. She wasn't expecting anyone. She looked at Emmy and found her friend grinning like the Cheshire cat. 'Crazy and desperate,' Emmy finished.

Melora's eyes widened with surprise. 'Desperate?'

Emmy didn't answer as she was already on her way to the door, Melora hard on her friend's heels. 'Is that Daniel? Is he here?' Even as the words came out, her entire body started to tremble with fear and uncertainty. Daniel? Here? At her place?

'He wanted to make sure you were home when he arrived. Dart and the twins went to pick them up from his hotel and dropped me here beforehand.'

Melora was astonished.

'It's only because we love you. We would never have interfered otherwise.'

'Well…you could have warned me a bit sooner.' Melora stood in front of her door, brushing down the jeans and pale pink shirt she was wearing. She checked her hair and looked at her bare feet. She was trying not to tremble, trying to remain calm and controlled, but it was becoming increasingly difficult. 'Do I look OK?'

'You look great,' Emmy encouraged. 'Open the door.'

'What if it's not him?' Melora whispered, her heart pounding wildly against her chest, her words drying up in her throat.

'Open the door and find out.' Emmy pointed to the door.

'Right. Right. I know you're right.' She breathed in, then out, before putting her hand on the handle and opening the door.

And there he stood. Simone was in his arms, and

he looked as though he'd aged a year in just a few days. His gaze met hers before quickly taking in the rest of her, lingering briefly on her lips before meeting her eyes once more.

'You're a sight for sore eyes,' he murmured softly.

'My eyes are sore, too, Daddy,' Simone piped up, wriggling from her father's grasp and almost throwing herself at Melora. Melora instantly enveloped the child, holding her close to her heart, breathing her in, kissing her cheeks.

'I've been missing you, Melora. I've cried at night and everything and then we flew on a plane because Daddy said we had to come and get you and tell you that we love you and think you're brilliant and— Ooh, Aunty Emmy!' Now that Simone had 'her Melora' back, it didn't take much to divert her attention. She scrambled from Melora's arms and ran to hug Emmy.

Melora was still stunned, still trying to take it all in. Daniel was here. He was here in Australia. He was in Sydney, in her apartment, standing before her. Daniel was here!

'Why don't Dart and I take Simone and the girls out for some ice cream? Give you two a bit of privacy,' Emmy suggested, and as Simone was more than happy to go with them, they all left.

Melora and Daniel didn't move for a split second before rational thought finally kicked in and Melora stepped back.

'Sorry. Please, come in,' she offered belatedly.

'Thanks.' Daniel came into her apartment, his hands in his pockets, feeling nervous yet determined. She led him past the kitchen and dining room into the lounge room and indicated a chair.

'Have a seat.'

'Thanks,' he said again, looking at the floor-to-ceiling bookshelves filled with all sorts of books, journals and magazines. A computer was set up on a small desk in the corner where the natural light shone in. The two-seater lounge was accompanied by two wingback chairs, a patterned rug in the middle of the floor with a coffee table on top. 'This is just the sort of room I imagined you'd have,' he murmured, not sitting down but rather looking slowly around the room.

'It is?'

'Yes.'

She was feeling highly self-conscious at him being in her home, his size and presence so commanding that he dwarfed the place. It was odd.

Standing here. Behaving like polite strangers. Him in his usual attire of shorts, shirt and boots, hair tied back, three-day growth on his face. He looked as wild and as rugged and as incredibly handsome as the first day they'd met.

He took his hands out of his pockets and rubbed them together before returning them to his pockets. 'It's a little cooler here than in Tarparnii.'

She nodded. 'You should have packed warmer clothes.'

'I don't own any.' He smiled then, that gorgeous, heart-melting smile, and Melora reached out a hand to one of the chairs in order to stop herself from falling over. 'Guess I should go buy some, given Simone and I are going to be staying for a while.'

Melora blinked twice. 'Staying?'

His smile was gorgeous and sexy and he was starting to slowly walk towards her and she wasn't sure what to do. Her knees would definitely give way if she tried to move. Her limbs were filled with tingles of anticipation as she watched him close the gap between them.

'Yes. Staying here. In Australia.'

'For Simone's education?'

He shrugged. 'Perhaps…but that's not why I'm here.'

'It's not?' She frowned, her mind unable to compute things due to his nearness.

'No.' He continued to advance slowly towards her, his gaze filled with need and longing and desire.

'Then…why?'

'For you.' He stood before her and put his hands onto her shoulders, looking down into her upturned face with a look of utter adoration in his eyes. 'I'm here for you. After watching you being taken away by that truck, watching as you disappeared from view, watching until the transport was out of sight and still being unable to move due to the constricting pain in my heart, proved to me that letting you go was completely the wrong thing to do.'

'It was?' The words were barely a whisper, her heart melting at what he was saying, her body capitulating at the way he was touching her.

'Simone said it all when you first opened the door, Melora. Neither of us have been able to sleep, both of us—more particularly me—have been so concerned and worried about you. I didn't hear anything from you after you'd left Tarparnii. I had no idea whether you'd arrived home safely, how you were feeling, whether or not your reconstructive surgery was still going ahead, how you were feeling about it all. I knew nothing and I was so beside myself that I took indefinite leave from PMA and flew here earlier this morning, desperate to be with you.'

'You took leave?'

'Yes. For you. So that I can be here for you when you go through your surgery.'

'You…you *want* to be here?'

'Of course I do, you silly, gorgeous woman.' With that, Daniel pulled her into his arms and Melora leaned against him, feeling the strength he exuded seeping deep into her body. Daniel was here. He'd come for her. He'd come specifically to be with her, to help her, to support her.

He looked down into her upturned face. 'I love you, Melora. I should have said it earlier but I didn't think you wanted to hear it.'

'You crazy man.' She smiled at him. 'How could you not think I would want to hear that when I love you so completely?'

'You do?' He seemed genuinely surprised at that.

'Yes. I've been miserable since I arrived home,

not wanting to do anything except return to Tarparnii to be with you and Simone.'

'You want to go back to Tarparnii?'

'Of course I do. I loved it there.'

'But your surgery?'

'Needs to happen. You said that our timing was off and I believed you.'

'I was wrong. Watching you go the other day proved that to me. Without you there, in my life, being an integral part of it…nothing else made any more sense. Not my job with PMA. Not Simone's education. None of it mattered at all if you weren't there by my side. My Melora. My *Separ.*'

'Oh, Daniel.'

After that, there was no more talking as he lowered his mouth to hers, claiming her lips in a kiss of promise…a promise that would last them a lifetime. This time, now that they'd declared their love for each other, there was no holding back.

'Ah…Melora, I think both of us have been a little crazy. Love seeped into us and we were too stunned to think clearly. At least, that's the way you make me feel.' He kissed her again. 'I have missed you so much. These past few days felt like for ever, especially when I couldn't contact you. I'd been notified by PMA that you'd been through your debriefing but apart from that—nothing. That's why I contacted Dart and Emmy, why I enlisted their help, because I simply had to know that you were all right.'

'I'm sorry I wasn't answering the phone. I was… upset. I didn't want to see anyone, talk to anyone… I just wanted you and Simone, and as I couldn't have you…I just shut myself off.'

'Oh, Mel.' He pressed another reassuring kiss to her lips. 'We're here now and we're never going to let you go again. After you left, my life was empty. I had everything I'd always had but until you arrived, I hadn't realised anything was missing. I know that probably doesn't make much sense but the way I feel about you, the deep abiding friendship as well as the intellectual link we share, not to mention that I find you incredibly sexy,' he added, brushing a quick kiss to her lips, 'is what I need to make my life complete. I've loved and lost once in my life and it was painful.' He slowly shook his head. 'But I lived through it. I have Simone and she is a constant blessing on my life. However, there is a void within both of us, a hole that only you can fill.'

Daniel released her but only so he could take her

hands in his as he knelt. Melora's eyes widened in astonishment.

'I apologise if this seems sudden but I know what I want—and that's you. Please, Melora, I humbly beg that you would do me the honour of becoming my *par'machkai*—my partner for life, my wife.'

'Daniel!' There were tears in her eyes, happy tears as she looked down at him. 'Are you sure? I have a few surgeries ahead of me and I don't want to be a burden to you.'

'Yes my beautiful *Separ*. Do you think that because that simpleton you were previously engaged to didn't want you because you've had cancer, I wouldn't?'

'I don't know, Daniel,' she answered honestly. 'My body is…well, it's deformed.'

He shook his head. 'That is only physical. To me, you are perfect.' When he realised she didn't quite believe him, he tried again. 'In Tarparnii we have a saying that roughly translates to mean even a goat with three legs is still a goat.'

'I'm a goat in this scenario?' She wasn't sure whether to be pleased or indignant. Her mind was whirring, trying to compute everything he'd told her.

'You're missing the point. Goats are very valuable

in Tarparnii. They provide mohair and milk as well as companionship and warmth in the cooler months, but a goat with three legs can still do what it was designed for. You may have been unfortunate to contract cancer but simply because a part of you has been removed, it doesn't mean you are not beautiful.' His words held power and meaning and she knew he meant every single word.

'It doesn't mean you are less "Melora Washington" than you were when you were first born and named. It doesn't mean that the endearment *Separ* doesn't fit you because it most certainly does. I want to be there, to support you, to protect you and keep you safe.' He rose to his feet, his words firm and direct. 'From that first day when I showed you the tree, split in two, with the new growth coming up through the middle, and you ended up in my arms—I've wanted you to stay there.'

Melora smiled, unable to believe she could really be this happy. Daniel was here. In Australia. Declaring his love and wanting her to marry him, to be with him, to become a family with him and Simone. 'And I wanted to stay. I want to support you, too, Daniel. Simone's education is important and I'll be with you whatever you decide.'

'Whatever *we* decide,' he corrected. 'You're

already like a mother to her, Melora. She loves you completely.'

'As I love her. I want to be with you and Simone for ever because, quite simply, you make me so very happy...and before I met you, I didn't think I'd ever find the one place in this world where I truly belonged.'

'It's here,' he said, enfolding her in his arms.

Melora rested her head against his chest, listening to his heart beating, sure and steadfast. Her own heart, which had been so empty and so lost not too long ago, was now filled to overflowing with love, hope and happiness simply because Daniel loved her.

EPILOGUE

LATER in the year, when they returned to Tarparnii, they were greeted warmly by their old friends. Simone had run off in search of her friends the instant the Jeep had come to a stop and as Emmy and Dart helped to unpack their bags, Jalak and Meeree came to greet them all.

Nahkala had come to visit Jalak and Meeree, as well as to attend a very special occasion.

'Melora. I am pleased to know that you have been able to keep the faith in you and Daniel and gain your happy ending. I am honoured to be accepting you into my family,' she said as she kissed both of Melora's cheeks. 'I did not think my Daniel would be blessed to find love twice in his lifetime but then you came and it was clear straight away that the two of you would one day be joined for ever, and now that day is here.'

The village itself was a hub of excited activity as people prepared for the annual *par'Mach* festival, the ceremony where two people were joined together, pledging their undying love and having their hands bound together in a symbol of unity, to thereafter be known as each other's *par'machkai.*

'Thank you for agreeing to have two weddings,' Daniel had murmured near her ear as he'd held her close and kissed her neck. They'd been married in Australia in a private ceremony with Emmy and Dart as their witnesses and Simone as their flower girl. This was to be their proper wedding, with all of their family and friends.

'I'll marry you as many times as I'm allowed to,' Melora replied, unable to believe how incredible it felt to be held by Daniel. She'd come through her recent surgery without any complications. Her surgeons were astounded at her rate of healing and Melora had put it all down to being ecstatically happy. 'That way I definitely know you're mine.'

'You, me, Simone and any other little blessings that come our way.' Daniel slipped his arms around his wife's waist. 'We are a family, my beautiful, intelligent Melora, and that's the way it's going to stay.'

Melora's sigh was filled with contentment as

she slightly turned her head to kiss her husband's lips. 'I love our life,' she whispered against his mouth.

'So do I, *Separ*. So do I.'

* * * * *